CRUSADE OF THE FORGOTTEN

PAT SHAND

JOE BOOKS LTD

Published simultaneously in the United States and Canada
by Joe Books Ltd, 489 College Street, Suite 203, Toronto, ON M6G 1A5

www.joebooks.com

Library and Archives Canada Cataloguing in Publication
information is available upon request.

ISBN 978-1-77275-543-5 (print)
ISBN 978-1-77275-544-2 (ebook)

First Joe Books edition: November 2017

MARVEL

Printed and bound in Canada

1 3 5 7 9 10 8 6 4 2

To my father. This one is for the good times.

THE OBSIDIAN TABLET

The All-Father of Asgard, clad in a sweeping, black garment of rich velvet and chain mail that glistened in the torchlight, dragged a sarcophagus down a tunnel he hadn't walked since he had forged it himself when the universe was younger. When *he* was younger. On this particular night, as he descended into the depths of Asgard's deepest chamber, Odin never felt more removed from that hopeful, young prince who had created this hidden prison.

He remembered his steady hands lighting the torches with a flame bewitched to burn forever, so that his future self might find his way if he ever had the misfortune to have need of a place this horrific. He thought he would be a good king, fair and humble. He would look after Asgard with strength matched in magnitude only by his compassion, and expected that Asgard would offer him the same in turn. Odin believed—he *knew*, as best as someone of his then meager years could have known—that this tunnel, this man-made hell, was a last resort . . . a recourse that he would only ever take in the rarest of situations.

The tunnel snaked below his beloved city as a reminder, to Odin, that there was always another way. That he was *above* it.

Until now.

Now, thousands of years later, as the heavy sarcophagus scraped against the stone path, Odin, father of the mighty Thor and the cunning Loki, felt neither strong nor compassionate. He felt tired.

Furious, thrashing thumps sounded from within the sarcophagus, which jerked in Odin's grip, but his fist remained clasped on its handle. He stared straight ahead as he descended farther along the path, deep into the belly of Asgard, miles under the kingdom that he had made into a home. He longed to be with his family at the palace, consoling them in their time of mourning.

No, Odin thought. *That isn't true at all.* He knew that soon *their* mourning would be over. It was only he, Odin, who would shoulder the burden of what had happened. Soon, everyone else would forget. It would be as if the attack on Asgard had never happened.

A muffled cry sounded from within the sarcophagus. Odin, his shining eyes locked ahead, remained silent as he approached his destination. If he stopped, even for a moment, he might collapse under the weight of regret. It was all his fault.

The winding, dimly lit path went on for miles, and he had

no company but those ragged, stifled screams. Soon, they would no longer be alone, king and prisoner. All those years ago, Odin hadn't merely left behind torches when he formed this subterranean chamber—he'd left an army of guards.

They rested now, but soon they'd wake.

The last torch flickered as Odin heaved the great weight of the sarcophagus forward into the darkness. Winding down into the abyss, the path opened into a platform beyond the reach of the fire's glow. Odin trudged forward, until he heard the sharp sound of metal on metal from above.

"Your name, Asgardian."

The voice boomed from all directions, its tone sharp with a note of accusation. Even still, for the first time in what felt like forever, Odin smiled bitterly. The voice was his own. He'd forgotten that he'd done that, and chuckled upon hearing his former self talk down to the man he'd become. After all, if that cheerful, cocky boy could see the All-Father now, there was no doubt he'd address him with unforgiving contempt.

"I am Odin."

"Your purpose?"

"I have come seeking the Obsidian Tablet," Odin bellowed, letting go of the sarcophagus's handle. The prisoner within slammed against the tomb, but Odin ignored it. "It has been lifetimes since I left it behind in this chamber, and Asgard has need of it once more."

"You understand, Asgardian, that once you carve the name upon its surface, there is no going back," the voice boomed. "Asgard shall never be the same."

Odin recalled shouting those words into the chamber as a young man, knowing that the only Asgardians who would ever potentially hear it would be him or his children. Neither Thor nor young Loki knew of this place, though, and Odin wouldn't have told them until his dying days. Now, though, he knew that he could never share the truth with his boys. His secret would die with him, or when Ragnarok came.

Whichever happened first.

"I accept!" Odin shouted. As his voice echoed throughout the chamber, a burning blue flame burst from above. Odin shielded his eye, now encircled in a glowing ring of light emanating from the seven giant suits of bewitched armor that stood around the platform, looking down at the All-Father with their glowing sapphire faces. None of them had the singular power of Odin's own creation, the Destroyer, a bewitched suit of armor that had the power to stand against even the strongest warriors in Asgard. This group of seven soldiers, forged from the Asgardian metal Uru and brought to life with the sole purpose of guarding the Obsidian Tablet, were enough to, together, prevent anyone, even Odin himself, from undoing what he was about to do. If any of his enemies were to find this chamber and attempt to release the monster trapped within the sarcophagus, these seven soldiers would guard the tomb with the power of Asgard. No one but Odin or an Odinson would ever be able to withstand their force or gain safe passage.

"May Asgard forgive you," the voice boomed. "And may Valhalla accept you."

The ground in front of Odin shifted. Tiles of stone slid back, revealing the item hidden within. Odin watched silently as the tiles continued to move, revealing before him a slab of stone so black that it seemed to swallow even the blazing blue light from the seven Uru soldiers. The stone tablet rose from the ground slowly until it stood straight up, reaching nearly Odin's height. It stood before him, a wall of black, thicker than the span of his arms and heavy enough to crush a dragon's skull.

The Obsidian Tablet.

Odin touched the smooth, unblemished surface of the tablet, looking at the dark reflection that peered back at him. In his black funeral garb, Odin looked like no more than a floating face—harsh, old. The black cap that covered his empty right eye socket looked like a hole in the vision that stared back at Odin from the tablet's surface. It had been so long since he'd seen it, in all of its terrible beauty.

The shrill scrape of the sarcophagus jerking across the stone floor shook Odin out of his reverie. He looked back at the tomb with growing contempt and grasped the Obsidian

Tablet on either side, lifting it up. There weren't many objects in Asgard that made the All-Father strain under their weight, but even the mighty king's knees buckled as he lifted the tablet. Its sharp sides dug into the flesh of his palms, cutting through the muscle. It hurt. He was glad for it.

Slowly, carefully, he set the Obsidian Tablet down on top of the sarcophagus, as the muffled shrieks from inside mounted. Odin grit his teeth and reached into his garment, his hands moving quickly so he would act before he changed his mind. He pulled from his funeral robes a crystal blade that glowed with golden power—stardust taken from Yggdrasil, the World Tree, used for only the most powerful of magic.

Odin stabbed the blade into the Obsidian Tablet, cutting through its perfect surface as if it were water. He began to carve the letters into the stone.

A name.

Odin stepped back from the Obsidian Tablet that now rested forever upon the sarcophagus, which no longer dragged on the floor or yielded muffled cries. The name carved upon the tablet's surface glowed lightly, catching the glistening tears that ran down the All-Father's face.

He rested a hand on the tablet, his eyes closed.

"I am sorry," he whispered.

With that, Odin turned his back on the name and strode away from the platform, back up to the path that led to the

Kingdom of Asgard. Although his family would still be in mourning when he returned to them, he knew it would be a new day for them. Their minds would be purged of what plagued them so, and only he, the All-Father, would bear the weight of memory.

As Odin ascended, leaving the chamber behind, the Uru soldiers fell idle, their shining sapphire lights diminishing to darkness. By the time Odin was gone, the only light in the chamber came from the name that glowed upon the Obsidian Tablet.

Sága.

CHAPTER ONE

CONTAINMENT

Thor Odinson, the Asgardian God of Thunder, held the glowing device in his powerful grasp, looking down at it through squinted eyes. A quizzical expression on his face, Thor examined the object carefully, but found that, upon closer inspection, it still boggled his mind.

"Stark, my friend . . . a question," Thor called, holding up the device with a muscular arm thicker than most men's chests. Thor had a square jaw rugged with stubble, and blond hair that spilled down to his broad shoulders. His voice was powerful, but also light and graceful, with an accent that couldn't be traced to anywhere on the planet Earth. He looked every bit the part of the god he was, his enormous form draped over Tony Stark's small Italian-leather couch as if it were a throne, but Thor's glinting blue eyes and playful, knowing smile were undeniably human. Thor pointed a beefy finger to a red icon on the screen he held. "What is this . . . this *Hot Flames Connections*?"

Tony Stark, sighing deeply, rolled in his swiveling lab

chair over to the couch on which Thor sat, and snatched his cell phone away from the thunder god. "What did I tell you about going through my phone? You might end up seeing something you don't like, and neither you nor I can take that back," Tony said. Tony's chin was darkened with a five o'clock shadow, and his eyes twitched from the continuous cups of coffee he'd poured himself since they'd been at work. Thor would say Tony looked tired, but the truth was, the man in the iron suit *always* looked tired, in or out of his armor.

Tony flipped the phone around and looked at the icon to which Thor pointed. "And it's an app. A new Stark app."

"What does this app do?" Thor asked.

Tony raised a brow at him. "Okay, scale of one to ten: how bored are you right now?"

"This scale of yours cannot *contain* my boredom, Stark!" Thor bellowed, leaning back in the couch until he sank into it. He had spent the past two days in Stark Tower, where he was "helping" his fellow Avengers, Tony Stark, also known as Iron Man, and Bruce Banner, otherwise known as the Hulk. The truth was, though, the assistance Thor was used to providing tended to be more along the lines of the *bashing-a-deadly-beast-in-the-skull-with-his-hammer* type of help. The *complete-a-perilous-journey-that-only-the-greatest-of-champions-can-survive* type of help. Even the *saving-the-world-from-his-wicked-brother-*

Loki's-duplicitous-schemes type of help. But this? Sitting and waiting while Stark and Banner worked on calculations, asking Thor questions that related to neither skull bashing *nor* epic journeys? No, *that* was not the kind of help Thor was used to providing.

"All right," Tony said, holding the phone up to Thor and tapping on the app's icon, opening it up. "Hot Flames Connections. You register. Answer a hundred questions about what you're looking for in a partner. For example: tall. Dark. Rich. Super hero. Avenger. Genius scientist, cuttingly handsome. That kind of thing."

"Hmmm," Thor said, peering at the screen. A beautiful woman with curly black hair and a kind smile posing in front of a bathroom mirror looked back at him. "I suspected at first that you were describing yourself, but the handsome part—I believe you fall short of . . ." Thor flashed a pearly white smile, "others present."

"All right—better example: pompous, unshaven, carries around a giant hammer? Could be overcompensating maybe just a little?" Tony said.

The truth was, Thor knew a great deal more about apps and software and Wi-Fi and smart phones than any Asgardian perhaps in the history of his people's existence . . . but that wasn't saying much.

Thor tuned back in to listen to the tail end of Tony's explanation. ". . . client enters that information, and then receives a database of all users within ten square miles ranked from best match to *yikes-seriously-don't-even-try-this-one*. It's a dating app that puts all of the work out there up front, so once you're set up, it's pure connection. One of my more soullessly capitalistic ideas, probably, but hey, dating's gone digital, so I might as well corner the market."

"And you keep this romance app on *your* phone," Thor said. "Pepper Potts knows of this, and you yet live to tell the tale?"

"Of course it's on my phone. On hers, too," Tony said. "I have to make sure it works. All Stark tech is enabled with all current apps. Doesn't mean I'm using it. Want me to load it onto *your* phone, man?"

"No, though it is . . . interesting," Thor said, his eyes drifting to the side of the laboratory, past a rotating display of Tony's previous Iron Man models, which gleamed scarlet and gold in the harsh light. In their many battles as the Avengers, a team of super heroes dedicated to defending the Earth from those who meant to do it harm, Thor had seen Stark don all of these incarnations of the suit, a weapon he wielded with power that could be considered nearly that of an Asgardian warrior. Though, of course, Thor thought with a chuckle, *Asgardians* didn't need a suit.

Thor's gaze moved beyond the suits and settled on Bruce Banner. He was coding on one of Tony's oversized computers, which displayed a digital projection in the center of the room. As Banner typed with increasing speed, his salt-and-pepper hair falling into his face, the projection began to swim with 1s and 0s. Thor had *no idea* what he was looking at.

"Interesting, huh?" Tony said. "You're asking me about *apps*, Thor. I couldn't imagine something that you're less interested in than the way my dating software works. Though—again, definitely going to corner that market, no one's even close to the user-friendly interface we use and—"

"Stark!" Thor bellowed, leaning toward Tony. "You speak true, my friend. I am not interested, though I commend your mastery of your skills. It's admirable. Relatively, of course. But my friend . . . how much *longer* do you think we'll be doing this?"

"Hm. One sec," Tony said. He spun on his swivel chair to face Banner. "Bruce! How much longer?"

Bruce grumbled, his fingers darting across the keyboard.

Tony turned back around to face Thor. "I'd interpret that grumble as anywhere from another *day* to another sixty years."

Thor slid farther down into the couch, groaning loudly. He knew for certain that there was adventure to be had in Asgard, and ached for the excitement it promised. Last he visited his home realm three days prior, there had been word of a ruthless creature prowling the lands said to be composed of millions of insects. Though no sightings had been confirmed within the bounds of the Asgardian king-dom, he had planned to set out in search of the monster with his friends the Warriors Three—Fandral the Dashing,

Hogun the Grim, and Volstagg the Voluminous—and the unstoppable warrior-goddess, Lady Sif. There were no finer soldiers in all of Asgard than those four except Thor himself, though some might argue that Sif gave Thor a run for his money. Thor might actually be among those arguing in Sif's favor, though he would never speak it aloud to his friend, lest he lose bragging rights.

While Sif and the others were back home engaged in what was sure to be a rousing battle with this insect demon, followed, no doubt, by a banquet that would make their ancestors proud, Thor was here, in a laboratory, doing work that he *knew* in his mind was important but didn't feel in his heart was such. Tony Stark and Bruce Banner had enlisted his aid in testing new hardware they were working on . . . something that had never been asked of the thunder god before. The device, dubbed the En-Trapp, was designed to capture and indefinitely hold immense amounts of energy, including but not limited to explosions, laser beams, bombs, fire, concentrated mystical force, and even alien beings. If successful, the En-Trapp would be the Avengers' way to take charge of damage control when super-powered foes attacked in heavily populated areas. Combating super villains head-on had led to destruction and devastation in the past, but if they were armed with a handheld device that could trap and incapacitate an attacker, they could curb any big threats before any damage could be done.

While today's tests had been nothing but mind-numbingly dull questions, at least yesterday's trials had been somewhat eventful. Thor never believed he'd look back longingly at an afternoon spent in the Avengers' training room blasting robotic devices to pieces, but even an Asgardian warrior couldn't overcome boredom.

The previous day, before Thor had known what part he'd be playing in the evaluation of the En-Trapps, he had convened in the training room with Iron Man, decked out in full armor, and Bruce Banner, who was watching from a desk off to the side. The room, right in the center of the enormous Stark Tower, was gigantic. Steve Rogers, the Avenger known as Captain America, had remarked upon seeing Tony's recent renovations that the room looked like a "baseball stadium." What intrigued Thor, though, was that its walls were padded with fireproof cushions, which allowed for some no-holds-barred training sessions with the Hulk that would've left their previous gym in flames when Thor summoned his thunder.

Before Thor could ask Tony what exactly they were going to do to the En-Trapps, one of Tony's old Iron Man models, piloted by F.R.I.D.A.Y.—the artificial intelligence that assisted him in controlling the suit, his tech, and keeping him from making bad decisions—carted in a large case of the devices. They were metallic orbs, each of them glowing a different color.

"Does each one possess a different power?" Thor asked.

"Nah," Iron Man said, his voice coming through the suit with a smooth, robotic din. "Got a little color code action going on to tell the software apart. Each of 'em do the same thing; it's just a matter of what system works better."

"We're essentially trying to contain the uncontainable," Banner said. "And to do that, we need a program that will utilize the renewable repulsor tech in a way that keeps volatile energy from making contact with the hardware."

"Ah," Thor said, nodding. "Next time, I shall resist the urge to ask."

Iron Man snickered and walked to the center of the training room. "If you think *that* was boring, whew, all I can say is that you better hope today goes better than expected." He cleared his throat. "Hit me, F.R.I.D.A.Y."

One of the En-Trapps, glowing with a hot-pink light, shot up into the air.

"Excellent," Thor said. "The color of your soul."

"Exactly. Neon, like Vegas pink, baby," Iron Man said. He held his gauntlet out toward the En-Trapp. The repulsor pod on his palm glowed brightly before discharging a beam of blazing blue power.

As the beam shot at the En-Trapp, the device expanded, stretching open into an intricate system of wires and layers and layers of metal, all of it snaked with veins of hot-pink energy. The open En-Trapp, moving faster than even

Thor could follow, shifted around the beam of Iron Man's repulsor energy, catching it in midair. The En-Trapp closed around the beam, condensing it, getting smaller and smaller until returning to its normal size and falling to the floor. It twitched once, twice, and then fell still.

"Excellent," Banner said, standing up with a clap. "I—I have to say, that's a fantastic start."

"The pink-coded program was one of my ideas," Iron Man said, tapping an armored finger against his temple. "Not that we're keeping track. Just speaking truths."

"Are we finished, then?" Thor asked, confused.

"Noooope," Iron Man said. He put a hand on Thor's back, ushering him forward. Stark whistled, and another pink-coded En-Trapp shot up from the pile.

"Perhaps a purple one for me?" Thor asked.

"We're not coloring, Thor. We're testing complicated algorithms," Iron Man said.

"Well, that doesn't mean we can't do purple next," Banner said.

Thor pointed Mjolnir at Banner, grinning widely. "My friend."

Iron Man chuckled as he pointed at the En-Trapp. "All right, purple boy. Wind up your hammer and smite that little bugger there as if it's a . . . what's that creature from your world? The one that smells like dumpster juice and Asiago cheese?"

"A Barglewarf," Thor said.

"Right, right," Iron Man said. "Blast the En-Trapp as if it were a Barglewarf. Give it all you've got."

Thor raised his eyebrows. "As you wish." He raised his hammer to the air and closed his eyes, feeling the residual energy gathered in its core from the last time he'd called down the lightning of Asgard. He spun the hammer, which crackled with veins of electricity. It became a blur of silver and flashing blue, getting faster and faster until, when it felt as if it had built enough energy to, indeed, blow a creature as massive—and, indeed, pungent—as a Barglewarf to pieces, Thor extended his arm and locked his hands around the hammer's handle. A mighty bolt of lightning burst from Mjolnir and sped toward the En-Trapp, which had already expanded to catch the blast.

The En-Trapp snapped in on Thor's lightning and began to reform into a sphere. It grew smaller and smaller, but didn't fall to the ground. Instead, once it was close to its original size, it vibrated in midair. Thor watched as the oscillations increased in speed until the entire En-Trapp was a blurring spot of purple in front of them.

Then, with an explosive crack of thunder, the En-Trapp exploded. Thor's lightning bolt blasted out in a flash of blinding light and sent the shattered plates of the device flying in all directions. Thor once again appreciated that the room was fireproof.

They tried again, this time with a blue one. It exploded, same as the previous one. On the third try, now with an En-Trapp that glowed orange like an ember, the device didn't even manage to close around Thor's bolt. Instead, it burst into flames upon impact.

"Hah!" Thor bellowed, holding his hammer high as Iron Man stared at him. "The power of the mighty Thor shall not be contained!"

"Definitely something to be proud of," Iron Man said. "On the other hand, what you might not know is that you're stuck here until the En-Trapp *can* contain your might."

Thor's face fell. "Apologies . . . what?"

Now, a full day later, which felt to Thor much more like a year, the God of Thunder was being subjected to a seemingly endless barrage of questions. *What substances have you seen withstand your lightning? Are Earth lightning and Asgardian lighting interchangeable?* They went on and on, which was bad enough, but now Banner was silently coding, leaving Thor with nothing but his thoughts and inquiries about Stark's dating app.

Finally, Bruce stood up, shaking out his hands as he walked over to Tony and Thor. He sighed and offered a wry, apologetic smile. "It's on auto now. Should finish up in about five minutes. We'll load the new programming into the next trial En-Trapp and go from there. I'm still thinking you're not going to have to make any physical changes to the hardware, Tony. You hear from Strange yet?"

Tony nodded. "Yeah, he finally texted back. He's all booked up today and the next few, but he's freed up at the end of the week. And hey, check this out." Tony held up the phone. "Who would've thought that the day would come when Doctor Strange sends an emoji? A thumbs-up emoji. Not as annoyingly playful as a smiley face, not as lifeless as a checkmark. I dig it. I would've maybe expected a crystal ball from the man, but I guess that's a little too on the nose."

"If we are to be locked in here for ages like prisoners forced into a life of mind-numbing labor, I anticipate Stephen Strange's arrival," Thor said, grinning. "He always comes with rousing tales of horrors unknown to the world at large. I believe he would make quite an impression at my father's royal dining hall. The tales of Strange's heroic encounters with the foul creature Shuma-Gorath would no doubt earn him his rightful place on an Asgardian tapestry."

"Tapestry qualifications aside, he's going to be another stellar test subject for this," Banner said. "If we can tweak this thing to contain Thor's power *and* the magic of the Sorcerer Supreme, then we're onto something."

Tony clicked his tongue. "I'm telling you, I know what he's gonna do."

"What is he going to do?" Thor asked.

"He won't," Banner said. "Strange, beyond being the Sorcerer Supreme, is a man of science. He respects other men of science. He won't do it."

"Do *what*?" Thor asked.

"He's gonna come in here," Tony said, grinning widely at Banner, who shook his head, "and he's gonna look at our careful calculations and precise programming with this— this pensive look, right? Thoughtful. Maybe he'll even cradle his chin. And, after a few compliments on what we've done, he's going to say, '*Hm.*' And then he'll crack into what I'm sure he considers a *helpful* diatribe about how a *spell* will give the En-Trapp the final boost it needs to work perfectly. He's done it to me hundreds of times."

"That sounds fantastic!" Thor said. "Perhaps we best put our work on hold and reconvene once Stephen Strange arrives to put this project to rest."

"No," Tony Stark and Bruce Banner both snapped at once.

Thor sighed. "Alas, the truth comes out. You want to keep me here forever as your science slave."

"Magic is . . ." Banner said, waving his hands around as he attempted to find the word. He always spoke slowly, precisely, controlling every word. It was no wonder to Thor that Banner was that way, considering how much time he spent out of control when he embraced the monster within. Banner continued, "Magic isn't unconditional, nor concrete. It's corruptible. We've seen it happen to Stephen. Spells go awry, magic can fester and change. That is no slight against what Doctor Strange does—his mastery of sorcery far eclipses mine of science *combined* with Tony's."

"Hey, now," Tony said. "Let's not get hyperbolic."

"But this," Banner said, gesturing toward the screen reconfiguring the En-Trapp's software. "This is meant to protect people in the long run. What it contains must *always* be contained, or we're going to end up blowing ourselves up down the line and unleashing hell upon the world we're trying to save."

"Remember the part about hyperbole?" Tony asked. "I did—I did just say that, right?"

"The point is, we need absolute, immovable calculations. I'm sorry you're stuck here, Thor. You have to know it's important," Banner said.

Thor nodded solemnly. "Aye. Can we order pizza?"

Before Tony or Bruce could respond, a red light flashed in the lab. Tony stood up like a shot and strode toward his armory. F.R.I.D.A.Y spoke through a sound system that boomed through the entire workshop.

"Known enemies of the Avengers have been spotted by a security camera in Brooklyn near Fulton and Bedford," F.R.I.D.A.Y. said. "Sending coordinates to your suit. There are confirmed injuries, but nothing mortal—yet."

Thor and Banner stood up, knowing without any further communication with one another that it was time to assemble. Thor held out his hand toward the corner of the room, where his weapon of choice—the hammer Mjolnir, forged of Uru and enchanted by his father, the Great Odin, to only respond to the hand that was worthy—was propped against the wall. The air thickened around Thor as the hammer responded to the call of its owner, shooting across the room and into the Asgardian warrior's open hand. Beyond blowing En-Trapps to bits, it had also guided Thor through some of the most challenging battles of his life. It was more than a weapon. Mjolnir was an extension of Thor, as much a part of the God of Thunder as the hand that grasped it.

"Who do we have?" Tony asked. He pulled off his T-shirt, walked toward his shining Iron Man suit, and began to snap it into place around his limbs.

"The Hood and Madame Masque have been confirmed by facial recognition software," F.R.I.D.A.Y. said. "As much as a woman in a mask *can* be confirmed."

"Ugh. My favorites," Tony said. Thor knew Stark had history with Madame Masque, and the Hood was a villain that had, at one point, turned from a street-level nuisance into a nearly apocalyptic demonic threat. "What are they up to?"

"I'm in the street camera, but I'm not getting a good look at them. There are three of them. They're chasing someone," F.R.I.D.A.Y. said.

"Let us act with haste, then," Thor said, nodding to Tony as the Iron Man faceplate snapped into place.

"Don't act all grim and stoic," Tony said. "Admit it, you're a *little* relieved."

Thor winked at him. "I'll allow myself to feel relieved

when we find out what's going on with our *friends* in Brooklyn."

"Yeah, yeah," Tony said, his voice taking on a slight robotic din now that he wore the full armor. He ran in stride with Thor and Banner to the elevator—already opened by F.R.I.D.A.Y.

"F.R.I.D.A.Y., is it a civilian they're after? I don't like the idea of a *group* of these clowns chasing after someone. *That* usually happens when crime factions start warring openly, and the last thing we need is super villains having a turf war in my city. I've had my fair share of organized crime drama lately, and I have to say, I'm not feeling it. What ever happened to a good old alien invasion?"

Thor flipped the hammer in his hand. "It matters not who they apprehend. If these scoundrels are in pursuit of someone, it falls on us to save—"

"I have visual confirmation on the target," F.R.I.D.A.Y. said, a note of hesitation in her computerized voice. "Loki."

CHAPTER TWO

HE LIES

An invisible stranger watched from the shadows, hidden to the others in the room. He'd been waiting in silence in the rank, abandoned auto-repair shop among rusting, broken car parts and discarded tools before the man and woman entered. A cruel smile spread across his lips.

"Could you have chosen a more repugnant place?" Madame Masque snapped, passing the invisible stranger whose leering grin remained unseen. "We used to call meetings in *mansions*. How do you think this is going to look to our candidates?"

The man who lurked in the dark had met Madame Masque before, and he found that nothing had changed since last they crossed paths. Even as she walked through this roach-infested, grease-stained pit, she stood with an air of nobility. Power. It made sense, after all, considering she was the daughter of Count Luchino Nefaria, the super-powered leader of the crime syndicate known as the Maggia. The stranger had heard they were estranged, but he didn't know if the rumor was true. Even without the weight of her father's power behind her, Masque was a force to be reckoned with. Tall and strong, she had hair black as the darkest nights of Jotunheim and was clad in a white and black nylon suit, perfect for combat. The only flash of color on the woman was her mask, a gold plate shaped to the contours of her face that covered her disfiguration. The scars on her face were a parting gift from Iron Man, after they'd had their first scuffle. She'd attacked him and he'd escaped, leaving her in the wreckage of a plane crash. When she emerged, she left Whitney Frost, the woman she had been, behind . . . and Madame Masque emerged. To this day, few called her by her given name, with the exception of present company.

"Really? I don't know, Whitney. I think this is the exact kind of place we should be doing this kind of thing," the Hood said. "I mean, you and I both know—we've made some mistakes, right? We had a good thing going, but we— we aligned ourselves with people who are all about the *I*, you know what I'm saying? The *me me me* of it all. There's nothing to shake the pride out of someone like crunching some roaches, okay? Whoever we can get to take us seriously considering the—considering the atmosphere, you know, then we *know* that's our guy."

The Hood was far more familiar to the lurking stranger than Masque was. While the stranger and Masque had met on a few occasions, the stranger had dealt personally with the

Hood many times in the past, when such alliances were less risky. The Hood was Parker Robbins, a man who came up as a petty criminal, a thief with delusions of grandeur who turned those delusions into reality by making a deal with the devil—or, in his case, a demon. The Hood had even worked directly under Norman Osborn, the former leader of the United States government branch of H.A.M.M.E.R., where Robbins used his position of power to target his enemies: the Avengers. He was defeated by what the stranger would describe as, perhaps, overstepping his boundaries—but that was all in the past. Here he was, looking formidable as ever in a zip-up hoodie and jeans, with the demonic cloak thrown over them. Though the stranger could sense that the cloak, which wavered on its own with no breeze in the room, no longer held the true force of the demon within, it was clear that leftover traces of the power remained. Without that tattered red cloak, Parker looked like nothing more than a man who leans against juke boxes at pool halls, looking for a mark to scam. In it, though, he was more than human.

Even if he sounded, to the stranger's ear, like a neurotic blowhard.

"Yeah, we don't need a big fancy mansion," the Hood said, wiping off a stool and taking a seat. He looked at Masque with a grin. "All we need now is each other, and patience."

"Are you sure it's not that we can no longer *afford* a 'big fancy mansion'?" Masque asked, looking down at him.

The stranger stifled a snicker.

"Hey, I'm transparent with you about the current situation, all right?" the Hood said, shrugging. "I know how we left things. Last time, everything was about *me*. You made it perfectly clear that—you know, that we have our own issues to get over. I'm asking if all of this works out maybe just think it over again, okay? Me and you."

From the shadows, the stranger grimaced, shaking his head. He came for a show, but he had *not* prepared himself to stomach relationship melodrama.

To his relief, Masque's response was cut off by a sharp knock on the pull-down door of the garage. She and the Hood looked to the door expectantly, but didn't say a word. A moment later, a metal slot in the center of the door clanked open and a small card shot inside. It slid across the floor, facedown.

The Hood glanced at the card and his eyes burned as his powers flared, making strands of dark hair blow off of his face. He extended his hand, and the card lifted off the ground, slowly at first. Then, it took off like a gunshot, zipping toward the Hood's hand. He snapped his fingers shut on the card and flipped it around to show Masque.

She looked at it from behind gleaming gold. "Queen of Spades."

The Hood nodded in approval. He glanced toward the pull-down door, which retracted, allowing dreary grey daylight to pour in, silhouetting the woman who stood in front of the open garage. She walked in and sniffed, her eyes squinting as she looked around.

"This your garage?" she asked, her eyes traveling around the room in near disbelief as the door clanked closed behind her. The stranger didn't recognize the woman. Her blonde hair was tied back in a black bandana and her nails were a deep crimson—all inconspicuous details. It was her outfit that made the stranger wonder, though. She wore a jacket and pants made from the same shimmering green material that made the stranger think of snakes. She didn't attempt to hide her contempt when she looked at the Hood. "Uh . . . nice place."

"Phononeutria, yeah?" the Hood asked, holding out a hand. She shook it. He gave it two aggressive jerks before letting go. "I'm pronouncing that right?"

Phononeutria turned to Masque. "This is legit? You're really Madame Masque?"

Though the lips of her mask were immovable, the stranger could tell from her playful tone that she was smirking behind it. "Yes, I'm really Madame Masque."

"Listen, I don't mean to insult your digs, but I thought you guys were running things," Phononeutria said. "The last folks I worked with, they may not have had all their priorities set straight, but they put me up right. After I earned it, of course. All I'm saying is that this doesn't exactly inspire confidence. I didn't bust out of S.H.I.E.L.D.'s custody to become a *henchman*, if that's what you're looking for. I want to do damage."

"And damage we will do," the Hood said. "Tell me, your powers—"

"It impresses me that you were able to escape custody," Masque cut in. "Your employers and coworkers within the Serpent Society weren't so lucky. What happened there?"

Ah, the stranger thought. *Of course.*

"A few of us made it out," Phononeutria said. "I'm loyal to the Society. They made me who I am today. The others . . . they purged the powers the Serpent Society gave them from their veins, and they gave up glory. There's nothing on the other side for me, and I depended on the scratch I had coming to me before the Avengers screwed everything up. They made *everything* fall apart, just as it was coming together. That's why you sought me out, isn't it? You want to take them down as much as I do."

"You're damn right," the Hood said. "If you agree to work with us, we can help you free your friends."

Masque turned to the Hood, her icy gaze boring into him, but he kept his eyes locked on Phononeutria, smiling widely.

She sniffed again. "Yeah. I'm into it if the money's right."

"We'll get to that," the Hood said. "I do believe we have our next guest coming up right about . . ."

The metal slot clanked open, and another playing card fell through. It somersaulted across the floor before falling flat. The Hood snapped his fingers, and the card rose into the air, rotating until it faced their way.

"Jack of Diamonds," Masque read.

The Hood clapped his hands together. "All right. I was hoping he'd show."

The pull-down door rose to reveal a tall, caped silhouette. The newcomer stepped forward into the dim light of the room without a word. He was clad in a black and orange battle suit with a utility belt around his waist that, along with two gigantic gun holsters, contained a surprising number of pouches—a leftover '90s villain trend for which the hidden stranger harbored a bit of affection. There was no doubt that within each pouch was a deadly weapon. A sweeping white hooded cape was draped over his shoulders, clinging to him like a caul, and the mask he wore was expertly crafted to resemble an anatomically correct human skull.

"Taskmaster," the Hood said, stepping forward with his hand extended. "I'm glad you could make it."

"Hold up," Taskmaster said, the lower jaw of the mask moving as he spoke.

He surveyed their surroundings, looking at the shambles of the shop from behind those dark sockets. After a prolonged moment of uncomfortable silence, he walked over to the side of the room, knelt to the floor, and, with a gloved hand, picked up a mousetrap with its intended victim pinned to the board, motionless. From the look of the thin, emaciated look of the creature's corpse, it looked like it had been there for some time.

"Yeah, to hell with *this*," Taskmaster said, and flicked the mousetrap toward the Hood. The Hood ducked to the side, and the trap landed next to the Jack of Diamonds card on the floor.

The stranger clamped his invisible hand over his mouth to prevent himself from bursting into a fit of laughter.

Taskmaster ducked out of the pull-down door as the Hood stared after him, his eyes burning. His nostrils flaring with rage, the Hood reached into his jacket and took a step toward the door.

"NO!" Masque snapped.

The Hood stopped in his place, but his hand remained in his jacket.

"Leave it be. We have bigger issues to attend to than ego," Masque said, her tone deadly. Her patience, the stranger could see, was wearing thin, as was his own. He was anxious to show himself, but wanted to make sure that everyone was accounted for first. Considering the sensitivity of his situation, he couldn't take any chances on being taken off guard by a wild card—so to speak.

The Hood spat on the ground, taking his hand out of his jacket. "Fine," he said. He turned to Phononeutria and

pointed at her, his frown picking up at the corners and lifting into a wormy grin. "You see that? You see how quickly
these fools pass up an opportunity?"

"I'm still not exactly sure what opportunity you're offer-
ing here," Phononeutria said. "I get to free my friends, get a
payday . . . but what's the plan? What's the big picture?"

"The Avengers," Madame Masque said. "The way we
understand it, you had a good thing going with the Serpent
Society. You hadn't even been active for a full year before
facing off with them, and you managed to do damage. We
want to give you the chance to do it again."

"I'm clear on what *I* can bring to the table," Phononeutria
said. "What about *you*?"

The Hood grabbed either side of his cloak and, with a
widening smile, floated slowly above Phononeutria and
Masque. Then, with a flourish of his cape, his disappeared.

"The hell?" Phononeutria snorted. "Nice parlor trick."

Madame Masque rolled her eyes. "Turn around."

Phononeutria looked over her shoulder just as the Hood
appeared behind her, a pistol held to her head. "Convincing
enough for you?"

Phononeutria snickered. "Kind of corny. But I can see
why you like that cloak."

"With your powers, my cloak, Masque's expert marks-
manship—you see where I'm going here, right?" the Hood
said, keeping the gun trained on her temple. "We're the anti-

Avengers, baby. And you know the only thing that *they* have that we don't have?"

"A place to meet that doesn't smell like a grease trap?"

"Weapons," the Hood said, lowering the gun with a chuckle. "Look at them—each of them. Thor is a god, and yet he needs a hammer. Captain Boy Scout, he's a super soldier but has that . . . that indestructible shield he likes to bash heads in with. Hawkeye, his bow. Iron Man, his suit. Black Widow—"

"Arguably her entire body," Masque piped in.

"We already have the cloak," the Hood said. "We build up a team, and we do it slow, play it smart . . . and then, we take their toys. Disarm the Avengers. Because you know what? They're not better than us. Not stronger. Not smarter. If we can even the playing field, we can take them out one by one."

"We have a lot to talk about before anything is set," Masque said. "Our plan is simple, and—most importantly—we're not rushing anything. We're focusing on building our numbers first and foremost, and making sure that new recruits ideologically line up with what we're building. It's not a corporation, not yet. We're not trying to monetize. We're planning to dominate."

"That's good," the Hood said, nodding. "Not trying to monetize, planning to dominate. I'm going to say that next time."

Masque glared at the Hood for a beat, and then continued.

"That's why we started off with a few select invites. As we build toward our goals, we'll expand. We want to build a tight-knit circle of like-minded individuals. You want the Avengers to pay for messing with your paychecks and your freedom? The Hood and I empathize with that, and we know for a fact that there are many others who do, too. Together, we can do this."

"We thought too big before," the Hood said, "We wanted *power*. The world. That whole thing. We have a different plan now. Once we're solid as a team, we're going to focus on these super-powered fools one by one. Start small. I mean, you almost took out Hawkeye last time you scrapped with these idiots, right? Why not start there? Imagine one of those freaky spores of yours on the end of an arrow. Pretty sick, huh?"

"No. Hawkeye is *nothing*. It's Tony Stark who should die first," Phononeutria said. "He is the worst of them."

"A woman after my own heart," Masque said.

"They *all* should burn," the Hood said. "And they will."

"I'm with it," Phononeutria said. "Is there anyone else on board yet? You keep saying we're starting small, but we should at *least* have one of us for every one of them, right?"

The Hood glanced toward the door, shrugging. "I invited a few more to start, but hey, their loss. Absorbing Man had a real chance at a glow up here, but I guess success just isn't for everyone, am I right?"

In answer to his question, the slot banged open and a

card shot in, whizzing all the way across the floor and stopping at his feet. The stranger grinned from the darkness,
pleased with his illusion.

"Oh," the Hood said, cringing. He lowered his voice to a
whisper. "You don't think he could've heard that from outside, right? Not that I'm scared, that just—that would be
awkward, you know what I'm saying?"

He flicked his fingers and the card floated into the air. As
soon as its back faced them, both he and Masque squinted
in confusion.

"What's this?" the Hood said. "I didn't send any of these
out. They should all be from the same deck."

Masque stepped up to the card, so it was mere inches
from her nose. "It's a tarot card."

The card slowly rotated until its face was revealed to her.
What looked to be a court jester rendered in a whimsical,
painted-art style leered at her from the card, juggling not
balls, but planets and stars.

"The hell is that?" the Hood asked. "A joker?"

"No," Masque said. "A trickster."

"Indeed," the stranger said in a deep, velvety voice. He
stepped out of the shadows, willing himself to materialize
into visible form, enjoying the gasp of surprise from the
small crowd as their faces turned to look at him. He stood
more than a head taller than anyone in the room, before
even accounting for the royal golden helmet that bore

curved horns that reached a foot and a half into the sky. He was clad in the finest black Asgardian leather adorned with golden straps, buckles, and armor at the knees, chest, and arms. An elegant green cape flowed from his shoulder armor to his boots, moving with his sleek form as he walked, his green eyes drinking in the nervous shock of the others in the garage. "Though, I'd ask the artist ... what business does a trickster have juggling the cosmos? Seems more the job of a god, don't you think?"

"Loki," the Hood said, his eyes burning with blue power.

"Parker," Loki growled. "It has been quite some time."

"Has it? Feels like yesterday that you sold me out and turned your back on our cause to help the Avengers. You're a traitor. A rat."

"Am I?" Loki asked, holding a finger in the air. He looked from the Hood to Phononeutria to Masque. He couldn't help but notice the fear in their eyes—they knew Loki, and what he did. Even Masque knew well enough to be tense. It was the Hood he'd have to work on, which was no surprise. It was the cloak that Loki wanted, after all. "I remember it differently. As I recall, you waited until I helped you gain more power, only to use that power to attack my home. *Asgard*."

"I had an *empire*," the Hood snapped. "You brought it down."

"I *died* because of you, but you don't see me moaning

about it," Loki said. It was true. The Hood's attack against Asgard had led to Loki's death and subsequent rebirth, and ever since, he'd been on *quite* a journey. He didn't know how much present company knew about his postresurrection antics. He wanted to control the outcome of this meeting and he knew he couldn't give them the chance to question him. "I listened in on your little *get together* here, and all I see is a repeat of your previous failure. A failure that wasn't borne out of any betrayal from me, but instead a flaw within *you*, Parker Robbins. You want to form a crime syndicate and yet have nothing to offer but a . . . what, a plan to *eventually* steal some weapons? No money, no location, none of your own powers anymore, no . . . *anything*. If you truly yearn to topple the Avengers and rebuild what you lost, you should listen to *me*."

"What's in it for you, glam rock?" the Hood snapped. "Because the last time I formed an alliance with you, like you said, you ended up *dead*. Who's to say the same won't happen again?"

"You must know what I want," Loki said. "It's been made clear to me that Asgard has no use for me. No place of honor, no throne, none of my promised glory. It all falls to *him*. My brother, Thor. And do you know what Thor cherishes above all?"

"His hammer?" Phononeutria wagered.

"*Earth*," Loki said, his lips curling with distaste. "The

brother who is promised the greatest kingdom in all of existence spends his days in this base realm, neither ruling nor exalting himself above humanity. I want to show Thor that if *he* can have what I so desperately want, I can *take* what he loves. I see your power, Parker Robbins, and I see what has drawn this group together. I wish to align myself with you so that we may work toward a dual purpose. When the Avengers fall, so, too, shall Thor."

The Hood smiled brightly. "I'll tell you what, Loki, you can sure as hell spit game. I just want to go around the room, ask my colleagues a question."

"Whitney, what's the last thing you heard about Loki?" the Hood asked.

"That he's running with the Young Avengers," she snapped. "With that little brat Kate Bishop among them."

"Now, now," Loki said, inwardly cursing. He was hoping word of his time as an Avenger hadn't reached all of his former allies, but it was nothing he couldn't handle. "That was a trying time for me. I'd been resurrected as a little boy, you see, but as you can witness, I've been restored to my normal state."

"How about you, Phononeutria?" the Hood asked.

"I heard Loki's not even an Asgardian. Supposedly, he's some freak Frost Giant that Thor's dad stole as a kid or something," she said. Then, as she looked Loki up and down, she added, "But he is hot."

Loki clenched his teeth.

"Know what *I* heard about Loki?" the Hood said. "This is a classic one. This is the first thing *everyone* learns about Loki. Any guesses?"

Silence.

"Loki . . . *lies*," the Hood said, pointing his gun at Loki. "He lies! Last time I trusted you, Loki, you lied to my face. Lied to all of us. I got *burned* because of you. Then the next time I see you, you're sneaking around in the dark like an insect, eavesdropping on my plans?"

"With offers to *help* you," Loki hissed. "Don't make a mistake you'll regret. *Remember*, Parker—you're mortal. Whatever vestiges of power remain in that cloak are but whispers. If a god wishes to align himself with your purposes, maybe do the thing that's in your best interest and *listen*."

"Oh yeah? I may be human . . . but that's for *now*!" the Hood snapped back, jabbing at the air with the gun. "I captured the powers of a true demon once, and I'll do it again! You shouldn't have shown yourself, Loki."

"What is your plan?" Loki said with a laugh. "To shoot me?"

"No," the Hood said, lowering the gun. "That's Phononeutria's job."

Before Loki could react, Phononeutria held out her arms toward him. Her flesh split open to reveal pulsating spores that glowed with a dull-green luminescence. Two shot out at Loki, faster than bullets.

Loki felt an explosion of scalding-hot liquid burrow into his chest. He let out a choked cry and fell forward, slamming hard onto the ground. He tried to gasp air in, but couldn't draw a full breath.

"You shouldn't have done that," Loki said, trying to force himself up. He closed his eyes, willing himself to blink out of sight, but it didn't work. He looked up at the Hood, once again pointing the gun at his head.

"Like I said," the Hood snarled. "You aren't going anywhere."

Loki forced a laugh. "What did you think this would do to me? I'm a *god*, you small creature. Now I'm going to make your *blood* boil, you repulsive, insignificant—"

The Hood fired his gun.

CHAPTER THREE

BROTHERLY LOVE

Thor flew through the brisk autumn air with Iron Man by his side, the Manhattan skyline stretching out behind them. As they soared over the East Village, Thor's mind was far from whatever mischief Loki was up to in Brooklyn. He had grown accustomed to perpetual uncertainty when it came to his brother. After lifetimes of betrayal, deceit, and pardons, Thor almost took comfort in the idea of seeing him again—because when he *didn't* see Loki out in the open, *that* was when he knew the Trickster was up to something truly nasty.

As Thor rocketed toward Brooklyn, he thought of the people down below. From all the way up there, far above even the skyscrapers, they were specks to his keen eye, no more than a swarm of color. Perhaps there was a time, too, when he thought them all alike. Petty and small, so far removed from the storied grandeur of Asgardian warriors, human. In time, Thor learned that there was no greater quality in all of the realms than humanity. Asgardians thought it noble to live a soldier's life, knowing that what they risked was nothing short of eternity. Humans were promised no such thing. They lived and loved and fought knowing that, in the blink of an eye, their lives would pass them by. And yet, Thor marveled, they strove to be better. To do *good*.

It was here, on Earth, that Thor learned how to be a hero. Because of that, and so much more, he would defend it until his last breath. Even against his own brother, he'd defend it.

"Got a lock on Loki," Iron Man called out to Thor as the wind whipped by. "Banner's close on the ground on his cute little moped. Very European, I dig it."

"Can you divine what Loki is doing?" Thor bellowed.

"Yeeeeep," Tony said. "He's on fire."

"I think I understand this one!" Thor shouted. "This means he's doing something with incredible skill. But what *is* it that he's doing?"

"What?"

"You said he's *on fire*," Thor said. "This is a colloquialism, yes?"

"Oh. Wow. Really?" Iron Man said. "No, Thor, he's literally on fire."

"Ahhhh," Thor said. "That sounds a lot more like Loki."

Loki promised himself that, the next time he had the chance, he'd rip that cloak off of Parker Robbins, and the man's head along with it.

Loki had been running through the streets of Brooklyn for a maddeningly long time, zigzagging through alleys and side streets in an attempt to lose the Hood, Masque, and Phononeutria. With the strength and speed of a god, Loki knew he could outrun Parker Robbins, but the Trickster had already taken four spores and two bullets . . . he counted himself lucky that he was able to gather the strength to run away.

Another spore rocketed past Loki's head. Loki cursed and changed directions, barreling down an alley behind a brownstone apartment.

"You can't hide from me, you rat!" Robbins barked from the distance.

Loki opened his mouth to retort, but stopped himself. He doubled back and bounced over a chain-link fence that led into yet another tiny alley, between a bodega and a Chinese restaurant. He ran past the dumpster, not daring to look back.

Loki knew if he could just get away from them and hide out for a while, he'd be able to overcome whatever poison was muting his power to phase out of sight and corporeality. His blood was working against the spores, which he was certain would have been fatal to any mortal. He just needed to actually lose the troublesome gibface before the Avengers caught them running around in plain sight. An encounter with his self-righteous brother was the *last* thing Loki needed.

As Loki was about to make it out of the alley and onto the sidewalk, he felt another wet stab of pain, this time in his neck. He spun from the momentum of the attack and fell to the ground, slamming his head hard on the concrete.

"Nailed him!" Phononeutria snarled, holding out her wrists.

Loki once again felt fresh poison spreading through his veins—and he would not succumb to this base power. He lunged forward, out of the alley and into the street, barreling directly into a man in a suit, who cast a glare his way until he, with widening eyes, registered Loki's appearance and took off in a full-tilt run.

Loki ran down the block, reaching to his neck to pull out Phononeutria's spore. It popped out with a wet, sucking sound, and as he heard the slap of boots on concrete behind him, he knew she'd have more for him. He gritted his teeth, turned around, and held out the spore toward the advancing villain. He tossed it at her feet.

"Time for you to die," Loki hissed.

A crushing, sudden pain shattered Loki's cheek as he flew off of the sidewalk and into the street. He heard cars squeal to stop from hitting him, but couldn't see anything but red.

"Really takes you off guard, not being able to—*boop!*— pop out of existence every time something's not going your way, doesn't it?" the Hood said, shaking his hand out. Car horns sounded around him as Loki's vision came back. He pawed the blood out of his eye just in time to see the Hood grab the car that had slammed its breaks to stop from hitting Loki.

The Hood's cape flared up and, holding on to the car by the hood, he levitated into the air. From within, an old woman screamed, her face white as a ghost as the Hood lifted her car off of the ground.

Phononeutria watched with pure glee as Madame Masque jogged up to the scene.

The cloak's power of flight holding him and the car up in the air, the Hood moved until the car, with the poor, shrieking wretch within, was positioned directly over Loki. "You're a *rat*, Loki. And I'm New York, baby! You know what we do with rats here?"

"If your current situation is to judge, I'd wager you live with them, you negligible, parasitic *virus*," Loki hissed.

"Wrong. We *crush* rats," the Hood said. He dropped the car.

What looked to Loki like a blur of crimson and gold zipped by the air above the car and then, a moment later, the vehicle was gone. The Hood stumbled to the side, jarred by the force of whatever had snatched the car from him. Both he and Loki looked to the sky, watching the car float away and disappear around a corner.

The Hood's face twisted into a sneering grimace. "Did you see that? What the—"

An all too familiar hammer cut through the air and slammed into the Hood's chest, lifting him off the ground like a weightless doll. The Hood's scream fell to silence as he disappeared from sight, rocketed away on the end of the only hammer Loki knew to have a name.

Mjolnir.

Loki scrambled to his feet as Thor came into sight. As much as Loki was taller than most humans he encountered, his brother was that much bigger than him. Thor landed with an impressive impact, sending a tremor through the streets and a boom of thunder through the darkening sky. As his red cape whipped around him and his blond hair flowed in the breeze, he looked every bit the god he was.

At this very moment, Thor was an angry god.

"Loki." Thor spoke the name as if it were a curse.

"Brother," Loki said, his voice dripping with sickly sweet sarcasm.

The red and gold blur cut through the sky again, slowing down as it approached the group. Iron Man came into sight, his gauntlets glowing with the dazzling repulsor power that Loki had been hit with more frequently than he cared to remember.

"The woman in the car—she is safe?" Thor asked.

"She's fine," Iron Man replied. "Makes me wonder, though. *Who* in their right mind would hit someone with a car that has a *person* in it? Even worse, who would *date* someone who would hit someone with a car that has a person in it?"

He looked to Madame Masque, who had twin pistols trained on him.

"Any thoughts, Whit?" Iron Man asked.

"The lowest of scum is worth ten of you," Masque growled.

"Missed you, too," Iron Man said.

"Aye," Thor said, pointing to Phononeutria. "I remember her. She infected Hawkeye with her wicked flowers."

"Spores!" Phononeutria barked. "And how *is* your little friend doing? I hear he almost died. *That* would've been sad."

"What brings you . . . uh . . . *varied* individuals together here today?" Iron Man said. He looked down at Loki, the slits in his face mask glowing. "I mean, not that I think a *We Hate Loki* club meeting is an entirely crazy idea. Loki, hi, always a displeasure."

"Metal man," Loki rasped with a grin.

Thor grabbed Loki by the back of the neck. "This ends. Whatever this is, it ends. We are returning to Asgard so I can contend with Loki. The rest of you will submit to Iron Man peacefully."

Madame Masque shook her head. "I'm thinking *not*."

"This does not have to be a fight," Thor said. "We haven't come here with the intention of hurting any of you. Again,

I ask you to lay your arms down and we can resolve this without violence."

"That's not going to happen, as you well know," Loki said, looking up at his brother, who returned his gaze with an icy-blue stare. "And they call *me* the God of Lies."

"Phononeutria," Madame Masque called.

The girl stepped up in front of Masque, facing off against Iron Man and Thor. "Been waiting for this."

"Odds aren't in your favor," Iron Man warned. "Step back, Phononeutria. Now."

"Yes, Madame Masque?" Phononeutria asked, a wiry smile spreading across her lips.

Madame Masque, her guns still pointed at Iron Man, said, "*Impress* me."

Phononeutria raised her arms, her skin moving as if bugs crawled under it. The oozing green slits of flesh pointed at Thor, Loki, and Iron Man as she readied another round of spores. They glowed as they prepared to burst from her skin and the ground shook as she reeled back her arms, ready to fling the spores their way. A dawning expression of horror took over her face, and Loki realized that the trembling ground had nothing to do with Phononeutria.

The Hulk barreled into her with massive green shoulders of pure muscle, roaring as he carried her away from the others, spores flying everywhere. Tall as a truck and thousands of times more powerful, the monster that dwelt within the

19A

VISIT **YETI.COM/REGISTER** TO LOCATE THIS LABEL ON YOUR PRODUCT. USE THE SERIAL NUMBER OR QR CODE ON THE LABEL TO COMPLETE THE PROCESS.

XXXXXXXXXX

This is an example only.

FSC

MIX
Paper
FSC® C144853

meek Bruce Banner was the perfect instrument of rage—an instrument that Loki had attempted to utilize himself in the past, which he knew made him not one of the Hulk's favorite people.

"I'm *not* impressed," Masque said, sneering as Phononeutria fell, still in the Hulk's grasp, unable to free herself.

"Hey, hey! Eyes up. Got the Hood coming in at two o'clock," Iron Man said as the Hulk held Phononeutria facedown on the ground, green sap pouring from her arms. Indeed, Tony was right—Parker Robbins flew down the street, the cloak whipping around him. "He's out for blood. Gonna need you for this one."

Thor held out his free hand, catching Mjolnir as it rocketed toward him, responding to his silent call. He twirled the hammer as he released Loki, his eyes boring into his brother's. "We are ages from finished, Brother. You would do well to stay within my sight."

Thor pointed the hammer forward and a blast of lighting came out, meeting the demonic flame in the air right before it would've hit them. The energies sent a pulse through the ground, knocking both Thor and the Hood back.

Thor rolled his shoulders and kicked off of the ground, flying toward the Hood with Iron Man by his side, as Madame Masque shot at them, bullets ricocheting off Iron Man's suit and Thor's armor.

"Parker!" Masque screamed. "It's time to go!"

"Little busy!" the Hood snapped back, shooting at Iron Man and Thor. From the way the first blast sent Thor backward, Loki knew that while the Hood couldn't stand against his brother, he would at least put up a fight for a moment. Which gave Loki the perfect opportunity to make his exit. Giving his brother a silent nod, he turned around and bolted out of there. He heard Masque scream his name, but he didn't stop. The moment Loki had enough distance from the Hood and the reach of his wretched powers, he'd disappear, and, to his pleasure, with neither Thor nor the Hood any wiser to his actual plan.

Thor stared at the Hood from across the street, his mind racing as he tried to come up with a plan to take the villain down as quickly as possible. Soon, police and emergency services would be on the scene, and the last thing Thor needed was men putting themselves in the line of danger for a fight that his brother had started.

"I shall take care of this," Thor bellowed to Iron Man, as the Hood came to a stop across the street from them. "You disarm Masque, Stark!"

"Hold up, why do you get to call the shots?" Iron Man said, but indeed turned around just in time for a bullet to strike his faceplate with a sharp *tink*.

"PARKER!" Masque screamed as Iron Man turned to her. "Come here and let's go!"

"YOU GO! Stark is coming for you! I *got* this," the Hood called as Thor circled around him, spinning his hammer. He pointed his gun at Thor. "I'm about to go one on one with the man, the myth, the legend. I've got to say, I expected you guys to arrive sooner. It's almost like you *wanted* me to kill your brother, but that couldn't be, right?"

Thor released the hammer and burst into action in its wake. Mjolnir curved up, knocking the Hood's chin into the air, opening up his body for a full attack. Thor struck the Hood's chest with his fist, caught the hammer as it came down, and slammed it into the Hood's stomach. The Hood went flying, but still somehow held on to the gun when he hit the brick wall next to a bodega. Inside, behind the glass, customers and employees watched the fight with wide eyes.

"Parker!" Masque screamed in the distance.

"*GO!*" the Hood barked again, his voice ragged as he stood to face Thor again.

"You care not for her," Thor said as he approached the Hood, who doubled over in pain, clutching his core. "You drag the one you claim to love down to the dirt with you time and time again, and yet you dare cast judgment upon my treatment of Loki?"

The Hood trembled before Thor, sinking to the ground. "I'm sorry—"

Thor reeled back his hammer, ready to strike. "Surrender. And tell me what it is that entangled your path with my brother's."

"I'm sorry—" the Hood repeated, looking up at Thor with a wicked grin, "—that you didn't get to say *good-bye* to him!"

The Hood disappeared, and then reappeared in a flash behind Thor, shoving the pistol into Thor's ear.

The sound was deafening, the pain instant. Thor, in disbelief that the Hood had been able to get a shot off, reached behind him at top speed and felt his meaty fist connect with the Hood's head. Parker was thrown clear across the street, where he slammed into a fire hydrant and landed in a crumpled pile.

Thor, wiping the blood off of his ear, felt the bullet lodged in his jaw muscle. A surface wound, but the pain in his ear from the gunshot was greater. Shaking his head, he pulled the bullet out and let it drop to the ground.

He knelt beside the unconscious villain, checking his pulse. Thor silently cursed himself for allowing his troubled mind to focus on Loki instead of the threat at hand—and again for, in his moment of surprise, lashing out. He could have very well killed the Hood, an action that Thor would never allow himself to forget. No matter what cloak he wore, Parker Robbins was a man.

Thor felt a pulse and breathed a sigh of relief. He looked at his fist, red where it had cracked the Hood, and was freshly reminded of the responsibility he shouldered as an Asgardian walking amongst humanity.

Iron Man rushed over. Behind him, Thor could see a

group of terrified policemen waiting for further instruction from the Avengers. Hulk hovered over Phononeutria, blocking her from shooting any more poisonous projectiles. The street around them was littered with what had to be hundreds of the withering spores that she'd surely been throwing at the Hulk but, like all other weapons, the spores were unable to break his impenetrable skin.

"Masque?" Thor asked.

"She took off. Ran into a crowd, disappeared. F.R.I.D.A.Y. is searching for her, but it seems as if she's good at holing up. Can't find her yet," Iron Man said. He cast his eyes to the ground and cringed at the Hood's unconscious form. "He's . . . he's okay, right?"

"Indeed. He lives. I know not how much of his actions are the fault of the man, and how much is the fault of the demons he keeps courting," Thor said. "But I believe the cloak is dormant, and will remain so until S.H.I.E.L.D. arrives to place him into custody. I must return to Asgard with Loki before the agents arrive."

Iron Man's mask snapped open, revealing a telling cringe. Thor knew exactly what his friend was going to say.

"Of course," Thor said with a deep sigh. "I expect no less from my brother."

"You sure you have to head out now, man? Masque is on the loose and so is Loki," Tony said. "I'm going to take to the skies, do a sweep. Just about an hour. You in?"

"No," Thor said. "I'll journey to my home realm even without Loki. If he is up to something, my people should know. I shall return before week's end to assist you and Banner in the completion of the En-Trapp."

Tony smiled. "You're probably relieved, right? A little excitement to break things up."

Thor exhaled deeply. "When it comes to my brother, my friend, there is no relief."

CHAPTER FOUR

THE LADY SIF

The Lady Sif grinned from the edge of the cliff, her eyes gleaming with excitement as the twenty-foot monster comprised entirely of stink-locusts took a lumbering step toward her. The brave Warriors Three—Fandral, Volstagg, and Hogun—were dealing with their own troubles on the lower rungs of the mountain where they had chased the foul beast. Even though each of the Asgardian combatants aimed for a seemingly vulnerable spot on the gigantic creature's body, they weren't prepared for the brute's ability to separate into multiple swarms. The stink-locusts that had been its right foot were attacking Fandral, as the left claw pursued Hogun, all while the tail wrapped around Volstagg's ample waist in an effort to push him off the mountain. Seeing their mistake, Sif climbed the mountain, forcing the creature to chase her. Scaling to towering heights, almost to the very top, she could see the road that led to the Asgardian kingdom in the distance until the creature, its skin crawling with the locusts, landed between her and the path back down the mountain. She did not know this mountain as well as those closer to the kingdom, as their pursuit of this odd beast had taken the Lady Sif and the Warriors Three to a barren, infertile stretch of unfamiliar land. Sif didn't know if this was the creature's home, or if it was merely where it had stopped to rest, but she did know one thing: if her plan didn't work, the only way off the mountain was directly *down*.

The beast lunged for her with wavering arms made up of snapping, hissing bugs. Sif closed her eyes, tightened her grasp on the sword, and ran toward the creature. She jumped over its swinging right arm and slid under its grasping left claw on her knees. Now past its hands, she sprung up onto her legs again and turned back to run full tilt toward the creature, raven hair blowing in the wind, pointed, silver headdress catching the light of the sun. With incredible momentum, she threw herself into the air for a mighty arcing leap, pulling back the sword as she rocketed toward the monster.

Sif penetrated the beast's chest, and he roared as the power of her lunge ground to a halt as the locusts collectively tried to push her out. Gritting her teeth, as to not let any of the buggers into her mouth, she lashed out her sword in all directions, praying silently to her ancestors that she knew what she was doing.

The first stab—nothing. The locusts bit at her arms, trying to pry off her silver and scarlet armor to cut into her chest.

The second stab—nothing. The beast thrashed about, slamming itself against the rock of the mountain. Sif had nothing to hold on to but the thousands upon thousands of insects attempting to push her out of the creature's body, but she knew that, if she fell now, she wouldn't be given the chance again.

The third stab—nothing. Dread filled her heart as the locusts clawed and bit at her face. She couldn't take much more before she'd have to emerge from the beast for a breath, something she knew she couldn't do.

The fourth stab—she felt, at first, resistance as she slammed her blade upward, the hilt held in both of her hands. Her eyes widening, she stabbed again, and again, in the same spot, until the tough resistance exploded in a shower of hot, foul liquid. As if she had broken a spell, the locusts dispersed, flowing away in separating swarms from the shriveled, bulbous creature on the end of Sif's sword. She recognized it as a Pupaetel, a parasitic creature known to suck mystical energies out of other creatures and use it for its own end. She'd never heard of one gaining enough power to create itself a body from stink-locusts, but then again, anything was possible in the realm of Asgard. Residual magical energy flew off of it in tendrils as Sif grinned, pleased with herself—but only for an instant.

The locusts flew away quickly, and the triumphant Lady Sif knew that she'd have to jump back down to the cliff before she had no more of the bugs to stand on, but when she looked down, she saw that the creature's efforts to get Sif out of its body had broken off the edge of the cliff.

Sif climbed down the locusts that remained, trying to circle back to the mountain path, but began to fall. The locusts were flying away too quickly for her to gain footing, and the only possible area for her to leap onto had been the edge of the cliff. She could try to swing around and catch the mountain with her sword, but she had a small window of time, as the avalanche of departing locusts gave her no time to think. She sprang forward, swinging her boots out in attempt to arch herself around to the mountain. With the grace of a dancer and the power of the mightiest of her kind, she swung her sword out as far as could reach. The blade's end scraped the face of the mountain, but did not penetrate it.

Then, with no locusts and no cliff, the Lady Sif, with the groaning Pupaetel still impaled on her blade, fell off of the strange mountain into the cloudy nothingness below.

Sif awoke to the distant sound of familiar voices calling her name. Surrounded by darkness and her body on fire with overwhelming pain, she panicked—perhaps she'd died and had awoken in Hela's infernal realm. As the clarity of consciousness spread, she got to her feet. Even though she was in agony, Sif looked around and saw that she was in no such place. She'd been to Hel, but here, she'd never laid foot.

Sif had fallen into a cavern within the mountain, but that was not what caught her interest. She stood upon a stone platform that led to a rocky path that broke off from the mountain walls and led into an opening. The path spiraled downward, lit by burning torches upon the cavern walls, until it disappeared from sight.

This was obviously not nature's whimsy. This, Sif marveled, had been built by hand.

"But whose?" she murmured to herself, taking a tentative step onto the path.

"*Sif!*" the call was distant, but distinct. Volstagg.

Sif looked up and saw three silhouettes leaning into the cavern high above her. Upon seeing the forms of the Warriors Three, cut out in front of dwindling sunshine, it all came back to her. The journey toward the barren mountains, the battle with the beast made from stinkbugs, and, at last, her fall.

"Aye!" Sif called. "I hear you, friends."

"Shall we send for help?" Fandral shouted.

Sif looked at the cavern wall. It was by no means smooth, but climbing it would be a perilous task even if she hadn't just fallen off of a mountain. Her muscles burned, her skin bled, and some of her ribs were surely shattered. She looked up at the Warriors Three, who, she knew, could be back with help by the next sunrise.

Sif knelt down and picked up her sword, sliding the withered Pupaetel off of it with her foot. Sheathing the sword, she made her way over to the cavern wall and felt the surface for the sturdiest rock. Her bloody, dirt-caked fingers clenched around a stone and she grinned.

"Sif!" Hogun called. "I shall journey back to Asgard and return with—"

"Wait," Sif said, hoisting herself up. Her foot locked into a hole in the rocky wall. She pulled herself up to the next stone, smaller than the last, but enough to grasp. She was in pain, and knew that the journey to the top would leave her in even worse agony, but there was no way she'd wait for a rescue team at the bottom of a pit. Just as certain as she slew the beast, she would rise and claim her victory. The pain wasn't a deterrent—it was a reminder that she was alive, and her opponent was not.

"Wait for what, Lady?" Volstagg bellowed, his voice echoing through the cavern.

Sif, hand over hand, foot over foot, ascended.

"For *me*."

After the long journey home, a bath to wash the blood from the countless bites and scratches on her arms and face, and a hearty meal to rebuild her energy, the Lady Sif, dressed in a white garment and silver headdress, entered Odin's throne room. She walked into the vast hall, adorned with gold as far as the eye could see, down the path that ramped up to the High Seat, where Odin the All-Father sat next to the queen, Frigga, who exuded power and grace, her smiling face framed by a crown of white hair. They were speaking to someone that Sif grinned upon seeing.

"Thor!" Sif called, spreading her arms as she approached the throne.

Thor, greeting her smile with one of his own, embraced her. When they parted, Sif walked up to Odin's throne and, bowing her head, knelt before the king and queen.

"Rise, Sif," Odin said, waving a hand clad in golden armor. Long, white hair spilled down his shoulders, mingling with his frosty beard. He gazed at Sif through a single eye, the same blue as that of his son Thor; the other eye, his right, was gone, the socket covered by a strapless patch. He had sacrificed it to gain infinite wisdom—a loss he shouldered proudly.

Sif rose to her feet and stepped back.

"The way I understand it, perhaps I should be bowing at your feet this day," Odin said. "Hogun, Volstagg, and Fandral tell quite the tale of your exploits against this beast. I ask for a moment of pause before we speak, Sif. Thor comes with ill tidings."

Thor shot Sif a brief smile, as if to ease her heart, but the look in his eyes worked to reverse his intent.

"Loki escaped before I could bring him to you, Father," Thor said. "His purpose in clashing with these scoundrels remains cloaked in shadow, but I know this: it bodes well for neither Midgard nor the Realm Eternal."

"What exactly happened, though?" Frigga asked, arching a brow. "Do you know for certain that Loki was acting maliciously? You did say that he was at odds with a group of villains."

"Yes," Thor said, his tone careful, "but past deeds lead me to believe that his intentions weren't altogether heroic."

"All we can do, as always, is keep our eyes open and our wits sharp," Odin replied, looking down at his son. Sif knew that it pained Odin, even after all these years, to treat Loki as a threat. He had raised Loki as his own, bringing him up alongside Thor. Loki once bore the surname Odinson and Sif would wager that both Odin and Thor hoped the day would come that Loki would do so again. Never would the day come, though, that either Asgardian would admit this, and Sif knew that rebuke from her king would be powerful if she were to suggest it.

"I will alert Heimdall as well," Thor said. "We would do well to trust in the stretch of his all-seeing eyes."

"A fine idea," Frigga said.

Thor turned to Sif with narrowed his eyes. He reached a

hand to her face, still marked with puckered wounds from the locust bites.

"It is nothing," Sif said, taking his hand in her own before he could brush her skin, still sore to the touch.

Thor's eyes lit up. "*Oh.* I hadn't heard, this relates to this creature! The swarm of insects!"

"Indeed," Sif said. She recounted her tale to Thor, Frigga, and Odin, pleased that at least one of the two hadn't heard a rushed version from the Warriors Three before she could describe in poetic detail her cunning triumph and stunning ascension from the cavern. Once she was done, satisfied by the look of admiration in Thor's eyes and approval in Odin's, she held a hand to her chin, pausing. "Wait a moment, there was something odd. Something I thought it wise to bring to your attention."

"Go on," Odin said.

"When I landed in the cavern, I found myself looking down at a path. A spiraling stone path that descended deep into the heart of the mountain, lit by torchlight as far as my eye could see," Sif said.

"In the barren lands?" Thor asked, his eyes widening with excitement.

"Yes," Sif said, feeling the corners of her lips curl into a smile. Of *course* the first thing that Thor thought of upon hearing this was adventure. "There are many mountains there, of course, but I remember the path to this particular one well. Perhaps, come dawn, we should set out to—"

"*NO!*"

Odin's deafening voice reverberated through the room, harsher with every echo. Sif and Thor looked at the All-Father, who had risen from his seat, the kindly look in his eye gone, replaced with sudden rage. Odin looked from Thor to Sif, his chest heaving. He opened his mouth to speak, his lips trembling as he did so. He blinked once, and then, slowly, lowered himself back into his throne.

"No," he repeated, this time quietly. "I forbid you to return to this mountain. I forbid any of you to cross into the barren lands from this day forward."

Frigga, her face pale, shifted uncomfortably next to Odin, looking downward.

"Father," Thor said, his face stricken with confusion. "Sif just related the tale of her journey to that exact place, to which you found no grievance committed. What has changed that—"

"Your king has spoken," Odin said, but the harshness was gone. He sounded, to Sif, tired, his gaze distant as he looked away from Thor.

Thor opened his mouth to speak again, but Sif pulled his hand away from the throne. She bowed her head once more to Odin. "My king. Your pardon?"

"Go," Odin said, nodding. "Get . . . get yourself a full night's rest, Sif. Your victory was hard fought."

"Yes, All-Father," Sif said, pulling Thor along with her.

Together, Sif and Thor walked out of the throne room and past the armored guard, who themselves looked unnerved by Odin's reaction. The All-Father could be prone to wrath when the situation called for it, but it seemed that he'd lost control of himself for a moment. In the quiet aftermath of his outburst, Sif could see his mind working behind his foggy eye, knowing that he'd played that card wrong. Thor and Sif were now more interested in that cavern than ever before.

The pair came to a stop outside of Thor's personal chambers, where the dazzling starlight reflected on the glassy surface of the pond. They glanced about to see if there was anyone within earshot, happy to find themselves alone.

"I've scarcely seen him so . . ." Thor struggled to find the word.

"Furious?" Sif suggested.

"Hah, no. His fury is as frequent as it is legendary. He appeared to be . . ." Thor trailed off, searching for the word. "*Shaken*. Odin knows of this cavern."

"I believe that he does," Sif said. "Though few walk the barren lands freely, we have also never been forbidden from them. I wonder if my battle with the Pupaetel opened a seal in the mountain, uncovering this hidden chamber."

"What do you think it holds?" Thor asked.

"I could not begin to fathom what would instill such a fit of panic within the All-Father," Sif said. "Whatever is in there, he does *not* want us to find out."

Thor looked down at Sif, another mischievous smile spreading across his lips. "He will expect us to break his word and attempt a quest by day's break."

"He most certainly will."

"Which means, my dear Sif, that we must not do so," Thor said.

Sif frowned, surprised. "I expected different words from you, Thor."

"What we must do is wait until enough time has elapsed so that Odin no longer suspects us, and *then* return to this mysterious cavern," Thor said, letting out an excited laugh that seemed, even for the God of Thunder, boyish.

Sif joined his laughter, nodding. "I am with you, as always."

Thor's toothy grin settled into a contented smile as he looked down at his and Sif's reflection in the still water. "As always."

He reached into Sif's hair and withdrew a shining locust shell. "You have a little something . . ."

"Oh!" Sif said, laughing loudly. "I'm sure I'll comb a swarm out of my hair tonight. I've never seen so many locusts, Thor. I couldn't have imagined so many existed within our entire realm."

"Is it horrible that I think your day sounds *incredible*?" Thor asked. "I would trade you in a second."

Thor's smile faltered, and Sif looked at him, her brow furrowed.

"You'll find Loki," she said. She held on to his hand, her eyes, too, settled on their image, shimmering in the lake.

"I know," Thor said. "That is, Lady Sif, half of the problem."

Loki, invisible to their eyes and undetectable to their senses, stood across the lake from Sif and Thor in astral form, secretly listening to their entire conversation. His physical body lay resting in the forest, tucked away out of sight from prying eyes, and guarded by mystical barriers that prevented even the meddlesome gaze of Heimdall from finding him. Though his physical form lay in rest, recuperating from the effects of Phononeutria's poisons, his astral projection crept around the Asgardian kingdom, learning all sorts of useful bits and bobs.

He learned that, come morning, everyone would be on the lookout for him.

He learned that his brother was still foolish enough to pass up a unique opportunity by waiting.

He learned that, way out in the barren lands there was something hidden that made Odin lose his wits, something that Loki, in all of his years had never seen before.

As he watched Thor and Sif part, each of them planning to return to their scheme in time, Loki stifled a snicker. He willed himself to return to his body and, one blink later, woke up, laughing in the woods.

He stood, brushed himself off, and, still laughing, made his way toward the barren lands.

"Sometimes, Thor," Loki said aloud, shaking his head, "you make this too easy."

CHAPTER FIVE

THE FORSAKEN AND THE FORGOTTEN

The next morning, Thor awoke as the sun began to shed its golden light over the Realm Eternal. He'd slept restlessly, with thoughts of his brother's schemes on his mind, plaguing his dreams. Too often had Loki's seemingly innocuous plans later blossomed into full-blown catastrophe, which gave the troubled Asgardian's mind ample fodder for his nightmares.

Now that dawn had arrived, Thor set out to meet Heimdall on the majestic Rainbow Bridge, known to Asgard as the Bifrost—the means by which one could travel to all corners of the cosmos. Today, though, Thor had no intention of making the journey across the cosmos. Heimdall, besides guarding the bridge, saw all. Even Loki could scarcely escape Heimdall's watching eyes.

As Thor approached the high gates leading out of Odin's fortress, he was stopped by an assembly of seven silent guards. They stood, blocking his way, their eyes locked again.

"What is the meaning of this?" Thor said, laughing. He

moved to squeeze through the line of his father's soldiers, but the armored men only tightened their ranks, creating a solid barrier with their shields.

With a scoff, Thor grabbed the shield of the guard closest to him. "Step aside, my friend, or I will demonstrate this day how to play the Midgard game of *frisbee*."

"Thor!"

Thor turned to see his father coming toward him from the castle, clad in war armor that closely resembled Thor's own, except with golden adornments instead of silver. The red cape spread out behind the god-king, moving in a way that almost made it seem alive. Odin caught up to Thor, looking at his son without scorn, but with unequivocal firmness.

"Do you, Son, disobey my orders?"

Thor raised a brow. "No, Father."

"Am I to believe, then, that you do not mean to travel to the barren lands?" Odin questioned. "Even though you, he who sleeps until midday, rise on this day along with the sun to set out about your tasks, whatever they be?"

"Aye," Thor said. "I have no intent to violate your word. I journey to the Bifrost to share words with Heimdall."

Odin nodded sharply. "A fine idea. I shall accompany you."

At once, the line of guards split, opening up a path for Odin and a baffled Thor, who followed behind, throwing the shield back at the guard he'd threatened with a frisbee lesson. The guard, startled, caught the shield between his armored hands, stumbling backward.

"There's your first lesson," Thor said, smirking as he stared at the guard from over his shoulder. "Tempt me to a second, and you will see your shield disappear into the sky."

"Come along," Odin snapped. "My men merely do what they're told."

"It appears, then, that they've been called to act as fools. Is this necessary, Father? Your actions speak to a lack of trust that I have not earned," Thor said.

"Lack of trust? Thor, you would do well to not let trivialities get the best of you," Odin said. "I think it wise to speak to Heimdall about Loki's suspicious activities. Is it so wrong to accompany my son on his short trip? You spend many days and nights in Midgard these days, and though you make Asgard proud with your heroics, I miss my son's step next to mine."

Thor studied his father's face and found no lie betrayed by the man's gaze. Just because Odin spoke true, though, did not mean he wasn't *also* keeping Thor from attempting to explore the secret hidden within the barren lands. For a moment, he resented his father for the implication that he would defy a direct order, before remembering that he *did* indeed intend to do *exactly* that—just not on this particular day.

Thor and Odin walked down the Bifrost, affectionately called the Rainbow Bridge for the way it shone with all colors, stretching across Asgard and into Heimdall's Observatory. From the observatory, with Heimdall's permission, Asgardians could use the Rainbow Bridge to access any of the Nine Worlds. Thor was perhaps its most frequent visitor, considering how often he traveled back and forth between Asgard and Earth.

In last night's haste to get to Odin with word of Loki's deeds the previous night, Thor had failed to exchange more than a "hello" with Heimdall upon returning to Asgard. If there was a soul in the realm who had seen if Loki had sneaked his way back into the Realm Eternal, it was the man on the Bifrost.

Heimdall stepped out of his observatory as Thor and Odin approached. He stood among the tallest of all of the warriors who fought in the name of Asgard, his proud chin inclined toward the shining sun. It was said that Heimdall was so in tune with Asgard that he could hear a blade of grass crunch underfoot from across the realm. Beyond these singular abilities, he was one of Odin's most trusted allies, a dear friend to Thor, and a brother to Sif. Thor hoped that he would act as a looking glass, allowing them to see the errant Trickster.

"All-Father," Heimdall said, bowing his head. "Thor. Your distress walks one step ahead of you, a force of its own. What plagues your minds and hearts?

"As ever, it is my son," Odin said, grasping Heimdall's hand. "Thor witnessed Loki in the midst of mischief on Midgard, and we hope to uncover the reason for his activities before he catches us unawares."

Heimdall looked at him from behind a horned, bronze helmet that cast a dark shadow over his eyes. They glinted like stars from the darkness. "That is all, my king?"

Odin narrowed his eyes and withdrew his hand, giving Heimdall a curt nod. He walked to the edge of the dazzling Rainbow Bridge and looked at the endless sea of clouds off to the side. They glowed amber as they crossed in front of the early morning sun.

"Yes," the great king said. "Loki seeks the hand of other like-minded individuals to do his bidding, but has instead found himself the target of their ire as well. When one walks on both sides, light one day and darkness the next, one may wake to discover that even trusted friends have become enemies overnight."

Thor stepped forward, casting a glance back at his father. Odin hadn't met his stare since they'd left the kingdom, which made Thor's already deep interest in the secret chamber hidden within the barren lands grow.

"Please, friend," Thor said, turning his eyes to Heimdall. "If you see anything . . ."

Heimdall sighed. "Loki has escaped my gaze—a cause for alarm, of course, but, as you know, commonplace for him. I do believe, though I cannot prove, that he has indeed returned to Asgard."

Thor looked at the shadow that covered Heimdall's eyes. "What makes you think that?"

"Last night. The moon," Heimdall said. "It shines *differently* when Loki treads under its watchful eye."

Loki had precious little time.

He knew that Odin must have sent a group of guards to the barren lands not long after Loki had set out the previous night under cover of darkness. Knowing the way his father worked, Loki would guess that Odin would wait until he was sure Thor was in bed before sending his men. At most, Loki had two to three hours on the guards.

Now, the sun warmed his back as he explored yet another mountain, searching for this secret crater. He had also cast seven astral forms to look while he, himself, explored, but, as of yet, he'd found nothing.

Confident that there was nothing to be found in this mountain, Loki spat with frustration and leapt to the stony ground below, kicking up a cloud of yellow dust. He strode across the sandy lands toward the next mountain—a jagged stone that shot up out of the ground like a severed bone, cracked in two. Loki imagined what he looked like from above, when the green of his garment was the only dash

of color in the entire barren, dried out stretch of land—
for now. One of the astral forms watched in the distance
as Odin's men—a squad of his six most trusted—marched
toward the barren lands. These were the men that Loki had
come into conflict with since his youth, the guards that
would alert Odin of any perceived wrongdoings that Loki
was up to. There were few souls in Asgard whose existence
infuriated Loki more—with two notable exceptions.

If he wanted to avoid open conflict with Odin's six soldiers, Loki would have time to explore only one more mountain himself. He hoped that, if he didn't uncover anything
himself, his astral forms would find something of interest
before their time ran out.

Loki scaled the mountain, running madly over its flat
surfaces, searching for any crevice that might match what
the Lady Sif had told Thor. Time wore thin, as did Loki's
patience, and he began to wonder if it would be better to
hang back and wait for Odin's men to arrive and lead him
right to whatever it was that was vexing his father.

Still, it would be better to find it himself, now. While the
men were no match for Loki, this secret mountain intrigued
the Trickster far too much to risk alerting Odin to his
schemes. Especially after his botched attempt on Midgard
to set his *real* plan into motion, Loki needed a win.

As Loki took a final trek around the mountain, he felt a
substantial crunch under his boot. Sneering, he pulled up his

foot to reveal the crushed, gooey remains of a stink-locust.

A wide grin spread across Loki's face.

He sprang from rock to rock, following a trail of slain stink-locusts, a manic laugh bubbling in the back of his throat as he leapt. He pictured Sif and the Warriors Three fighting the beast made from the creatures, slaying bugs with every swipe of their swords but not finding the core of their problem until—

Loki looked up and saw what looked to have been a cliff, its tip broken. All of the rocks around it were jagged, but most of the rock was brown, dusty, and sanded down. The broken cliff here looked like a raw wound, with red clay at the center. It was fresh.

Loki imagined the beast breaking off the stone surface, and lowered his gaze, following what the path of the rock would have been. He looked under the boulder on which he stood down to what had been a sealed rock surface that now had a cavernous hole smashed into it. All around, there were pebbles and chunks of rocks.

"*Yes*," he hissed and, without hesitation, tucked up his legs and jumped into the hole. He shot downward, his emerald cape whipping around him like wings.

Loki landed gracefully on bent legs, cape settling around him. Looking around, he found himself in the exact stone chamber that Sif had described. The jagged chamber of rocks above had led down to a small platform of stone, on which Loki stood. The platform then arched out into a winding stone path that snaked down like a child's slide into what seemed like an endless abyss. To Loki's eye, it looked as if he stood before a hole in the center of Asgard.

It was colder down here, despite the torches that lined the cavern wall, spiraling down along the curve of the rocky path. Curious. Loki, eager to discover what set his father into such a fit of uncharacteristic sloppiness, walked the curving stone path, descending into the heart of the mountain. He hurried, knowing that, by now, Odin's men were already in the barren lands, surely approaching this very mountain.

Loki passed the last torch along the stone path, which had wound down into a pit of impenetrable darkness, even to Loki's keen eye, and opened up into a platform beyond the reach of the fire's glow from above. Loki walked forward, stepping with caution, until he heard the sharp sound of metal on metal from above.

"Your name, Asgardian."

His father's voice came from all around, as if the mountain itself spoke to Loki, who didn't miss the accusatory tone in the words. How *like* Odin, Loki thought.

The Trickster spread his arms, grinning widely. "I am the son of Odin."

"Your name, Asgardian."

Loki sneered, feeling like he'd been swallowed up by the mountain from the way the voice rumbled the stone beneath him. He wondered how quickly he could blip out of corpo-reality if the mountain decided that he was a trespasser and to vomit him up. He'd expected a magical defense, after all, but knew that he had a limited window in which to act.

"I am Loki."

After a pause, the voice moved to the next question, seemingly satisfied. "Your purpose?"

Loki bit his lip, thinking. The cavern hadn't expelled him upon learning his name, which made him wonder if this secret might have been older than even he'd suspected. Per-haps it came from a time when Odin, in all of his willful ignorance, knew Loki as nothing more than a son, beloved though neglected.

"I," Loki said, "am the son of Odin, and come into this, his chamber, on his word."

Silence answered.

"I," Loki shouted, "am Loki Odinson!"

As his voice called throughout the chamber, Loki listened to it echo a name he hadn't spoken for long time. One that he thought he'd never speak again. It felt bitter on his tongue.

A burning blue flame burst from above, casting a blind-ing light down on Loki. Loki looked around the platform, seeing that he was now encircled in a glowing ring of sap-phire light. Standing above Loki were the sources of the flames: seven giant suits of bewitched armor that loomed over on the trickster god. The blazing light that came from the suits appeared powerful enough to reduce Loki to cinders if they looked directly at him but, instead, they just lit the path.

"Ah," Loki said, looking up at the armor. "Destroyers."

He took a closer look and found them smaller than the genuine article that guarded his father's most precious chambers. The armor was older too, forged in a style that he'd only seen in ancient Asgardian tapestries.

Loki suspected that they were early attempts at the perfection that Odin would go on to create with the Destroyer. The thought made Loki again wonder exactly how old the secret hidden within this chamber was.

"Journey forth," Odin's voice boomed, and Loki noticed now that it came not from the walls of the mountain itself, but from the armor. Not only were they bewitched with the blazing blue flames, but with Odin's words as well. "May Asgard forgive you. And may Valhalla accept you."

"I do believe my chances of *that* have withered, but I appreciate the thought," Loki said. As Odin's wayward son stepped forward, wondering what he had to do next, he received the answer as the ground before him wavered with enchantment, and something rose from within.

A large, ancient sarcophagus laid on the ground before Loki. The God of Lies had seen many Asgardians die, but it had been a long while since such craftsmanship was put into their tombs. That wasn't the strangest part of this magical tomb as Loki gazed upon a gigantic, black tablet balanced on the sarcophagus's face.

A single word was emblazoned upon the tablet. The glowing text pulsed with life, growing lighter and darker as if matching the beat of a heart.

Loki touched the surface of the tablet, expecting cool stone. Instead, it was warm. Warmer than his touch. He traced his fingers up to the glowing word carved into the surface. Running his hand over the indent of the word, he spoke it aloud, to himself.

"*Sága.*"

The moment his lips formed the word, the tablet burst into chunks of perfectly black stone, sending a shock of magical power through Loki's hand. Loki jerked his arm back and noticed a river of red flowing from his palm. The explosion of the stone had cut him to the muscle. As he examined the cut, he heard a deep scraping coming from inside the tomb. Forgetting the pain, his poison-green eyes widened as the lid of the sarcophagus slowly shifted to the side.

"Oh," he said, fascinated.

Of *course* something was within, but Loki had thought it was likely to be the corpse of one of Odin's old enemies, buried with older secrets. Some of the nastier threats that Asgard had faced had a tendency to rise from the dead, so Loki understood his father's precautions.

The thought hadn't crossed his mind that whoever was within the sarcophagus might be *alive*.

The lid scraped slowly to the side until it teetered on the edge and then fell, clattering to the stone platform with a sound that echoed through the pit. Loki couldn't help but let out a giddy chirp when a gloved hand reached from the sarcophagus and curled around the sides. Another hand shot out, quickly this time, and grasped the other side. Painstakingly, a shuddering figure pushed itself out of the casket.

Long, roped hair framed a gaunt face. Loki strained to get a better look, and almost took a step forward, but caught himself at the last moment. For all he knew, he could have just unleashed the very embodiment of Ragnarok, so he kept at a safe distance until he could share words with the creature.

The figure took a step forward, and the blue light of the Uru armor revealed a woman clad in dented, bloodstained battle armor. Asgardian armor. Armed with neither sword nor knife, the sheath on her leather belt was empty, and she held no shield to match her armor. She stood taller than Loki, with powerful muscles that showed through the broken, missing pieces of her armor. It looked as if she'd been through a hundred-year war.

Her eyes were milky and pale, perhaps blind, but still she scanned the area before her. She opened her mouth and let out a guttural sound, like an infant trying to form its first words.

Loki cleared his throat.

The woman's face snapped toward him. She croaked out another animalistic gurgle before falling into a fit of coughing. Loki felt a sudden, indescribable urge to run to her side as she knelt, her body shaking as she sputtered. The Trickster narrowed his eyes, alarmed by his own strange impulse. He remained where he stood.

Saliva dripping from her mouth, the bloody woman looked up. Now that he looked her directly in the eye, Loki could see the ghost of an iris and a pupil, faded though they were. He no longer wondered if she was blind. She looked right at him.

"Loki," she rasped.

CHAPTER SIX
SÁGA

That night, Thor awoke to screams.

As he darted up in bed, Mjolnir flying into his open palm from across his quarters, he paused. The faint, pained yowls that had woken him were replaced with the heavy silence of a peaceful Asgardian night—maybe he had been dreaming.

Then came another agonized yelp, cut short as soon as it sounded. It wasn't far away, either—just outside the castle.

Thor grabbed his armor, throwing it on haphazardly as he hurried down the corridor. On the way, he dodged around a group of Odin's guards marching through the hall in the direction of the courtyard. Thor, his heart hammering in his chest as he imagined what his brother had done now, picked up speed and raced to the throne room.

It didn't surprise Thor to find Odin also wearing his battle gear, surrounded by a battalion of solders. Next to the All-Father, Frigga held a sword of her own, a look in her blue eyes that Thor recognized: it was the same expression she'd worn when Loki attacked the capital city. A fierce, deep sadness.

"He's made himself known, then?" Thor asked, as Odin walked away from him without a word, toward a burly guard that knelt before the All-Father, presenting a bladed golden scepter.

Thor narrowed his eyes and turned to Frigga, whose hand tightly grasped the hilt of her blade. Frigga loved Loki most out of all of them, and Thor knew she hoped for a day when he would return, not as a bringer of war, death, and lies, but as her son. She'd hardly strike the Trickster with her hand, let alone a blade.

Still, she clutched it, her knuckles bone white.

"What has he done?" Thor asked, his tone hushed.

Slowly, Thor turned his head toward Odin, who held his scepter at the ready. Even more dangerous than the scepter was the burning glare in Odin's eyes as he looked at Thor.

"Tell me the truth," Odin hissed, slow and vicious. "Did you do it?"

"Do *what*?" Thor asked.

"Did you disobey me?" Odin shouted. "Did you and Sif go against my word and act on foolishness that I expressly forbade?"

The battalion of guards stood around them, clutching their weapons, looking away from the screaming All-Father.

Normally, Thor was able to maintain respect for his king even when he incensed Thor in a way only a father could. Thor did not temper his words this time.

"Are you mad, old man?" he barked. "I walked with you, as a *child* does with his doting father, on all my errands today. I ate and drank with your eyes on my back like I was a prisoner, and then I retired to my chamber to rest. What, Father, could I have done? And when?"

The All-Father looked at Thor, the fury draining from his face. An exhausted Odin bowed his head. It wasn't an apology, but Thor knew what it meant. *That* scared him more than any wrathful retort.

"We are under attack," Odin said, his tone hushed. He turned toward the hall, walking with purpose. "Come, boy."

Thor stood as still as the statues of ancestors past that lined their halls. He looked at Odin through narrowed eyes, and snarled the word: "Who?"

"An unseen foe," Odin said, waving his arm impatiently, expecting Thor to follow. "The attacker strikes so quickly that none of the guards have been able to catch a glimpse of its face. Four of my men have fallen, six more injured."

Thor approached Frigga, who gritted her teeth as tightly as she clutched her sword. She normally looked like a goddess in any room that she occupied, standing head and shoulders above even the mightiest warriors. Now, in the cavernous throne room, she appeared small.

"Mother," Thor said. "Who is this foe?"

Frigga opened her mouth to reply, but stopped, as if she couldn't find the words.

Odin turned around, casting a glare over his shoulder. "Now, Thor!"

"Who?" Thor repeated the word, looking at his mother.

"I—" Frigga said, her eyes searching. "I thought she was a dream."

"She," Thor marked.

"*ENOUGH!*" Odin roared. "For every moment wasted on words, another Asgardian may fall."

Thor touched his mother's shoulder and, without another word, joined his father. The All-Father and the mighty God of Thunder walked down the royal hall toward the exit, each swelling with anger at the other, and each ready to defend the Realm Eternal to their final breaths.

"I will reveal all to you, my Son," Odin said, his voice still harsh, though Thor could see in the man's eyes he meant to ease the tension. "But until that time comes, you must follow my orders without question. Do you understand?"

Thor gritted his teeth, but nodded. "Aye."

They opened the doors and were met by the Warriors Three and the Lady Sif, each armored up and prepared to do battle. They looked even more confused than Thor as they knelt before Odin, waiting for direction from their king.

"You have been made aware of the situation?" Odin asked.

"Indeed, though, I must admit the guard who woke me, besides being a little rougher than I would've liked, was quite vague," Fandral said, cupping his beard, the short blond hair sticking through his gloved fingers. "We were told to get our weapons and that—"

"The kingdom is under siege by a singular force," Sif said. "We're here to stop that force."

"And stop it we shall," Hogun said.

Volstagg yawned.

Odin stared at him, unblinkingly.

"Oh!" Volstagg said, raising his bushy red eyebrows. "Yes, yes. No one shall get past Volstagg the Voluminous and the Warriors Three. And especially not Lady Sif, Slayer of the Stink-Locusts!"

"I've heard better epithets given to hounds," Sif said. "Perhaps I'll call you Volstagg, Destroyer of the Dessert."

"A fine idea!" Volstagg said.

"Keep a keen eye, and stay close to each other. You must guard this entrance to the castle at all costs," Odin said. "Our attacker must not breach these doors. Do you understand?"

"Aye."

Odin strode forward toward the gate, but Thor looked back at his friends. "It's a woman," Thor said. "The assailant is a woman."

He held Sif's gaze for a moment before turning around, heading back to walk in pace with Odin.

"Father," Thor said.

"Yes."

"My love for Sif, Volstagg, Hogun, and Fandral eclipses in size and depth even the endless cosmos of the World Tree itself," Thor said. "If they die in battle with someone whose name you fail to share for reasons unknown, their blood will be on your hands."

Odin looked at Thor, his eye wide. "It will be on all of ours."

Thor narrowed his eyes. "What does that mean?"

Odin opened the gate to one of his personal flight crafts waiting outside, floating slightly above the ground. It bore a resemblance to the design of Thor's helmet—a silver body with an end that flared out and curved back like the helmet's wings. These crafts were able to fly at speeds unseen by those on Earth—most of them, anyway.

"I'd be interested to see what improvements, if any, Tony Stark would make on this Asgardian technology," Thor said. "Perhaps even the All-Father can learn something from the mortals of Earth."

"I have had my fill of your pithy comments, Thor," Odin said. "Follow me in silence."

"Of course, you'd never let a human tinker with your crafts," Thor said. "You trust no one who doesn't kneel before you, of course—and even those who do, even your blood, aren't worthy of the truth."

A battalion of gold-clad guards encircled the craft, parting as Odin walked toward it and hoisted himself up.

"You speak of a situation you know *nothing* about," Odin said. "And these crafts, in the wrong hands, as with all things powerful, could become a weapon. You see the situation in Asgard, Thor. Abandon your petty assumptions about my intentions and focus on saving the people who look to you for direction."

"*The wrong hands*," Thor repeated, nodding as he followed Odin onto the ship. "A phrase that, until recently, you've reserved for Loki. Who *else* do you fear would take advantage of such a weapon?"

Odin took the wheel and the ship lifted farther off of the ground, taking off into the night sky.

"Because I don't believe that you mean 'Tony Stark' when you say that," Thor said. "Who is this mystery woman Mother spoke of?"

Odin didn't reply. Thor noticed, though, that the ship flew toward the barren lands. Thor stood, clenching his fist around Mjolnir, feeling the need to strike something as soon as possible. He'd never been so enraged with his father.

Just as Thor was about to throw out another comment that he was sure Odin would consider "pithy," the All-Father spoke.

"Before . . . before we arrive, Thor, there's something I need you to know," he said with his back turned as the craft picked up speed, rocketing them through the starry night. They stood on its boatlike surface, the wind whipping their hair and beards back. The stars looked like streaks of light.

"Yes?"

"I never meant for this to happen," Odin whispered. "I never meant for any of it."

Asgard was nothing like she remembered it. Not the smell, not the skyline, not the way the stars looked down upon its splendor. The air was foul to her senses, overpowering and sticky with heat. Odin had robbed her of her time, and time had robbed her of the place she called home. It was gone, replaced with a strange land, unfamiliar and abhorrent.

All the better for what she had planned.

She looked down at her blade, dripping red with the blood of the last guard she'd slain. They were slow, in their heavy armor, guarding what she knew laid behind their ranks within the cursed All-Father's secret rooms. Oh, she would get it. And then, they would all know her name, as Loki now did.

And they, like Loki, would pay.

Sága crept through the darkness of the forest, silent on her feet as she watched guards clank noisily through the trees across from her in hopes of finding her. If they came too close, like the others, they wouldn't have time to react.

Ages of stifled anger made her quicker than ever, and stronger to match, and that energy was bursting out of her, never to be contained again. The world slowed down, grinding itself to a near halt as she jumped into action.

Through the cloak of the trees, Sága peered toward the front entrance of the castle and saw that four warriors had arrived since she'd last circled. She recognized them and found a pained smile flit across her cracked lips. It was gone as soon as it came, though, as she remembered her final moments with them—the Warriors Three. Worse yet, her sister in arms, the Lady Sif.

Sif stood, sword at the ready in perfect form. Always perfect. Always the best, brightest, and strongest.

That was then, and all of Asgard had changed, Sága and Sif included. It was time, Sága thought, to see how much. With her eyes locked on Sif, she charged from the thick of the woods and barreled toward Odin's castle, the sword of a slain guard in her hand, stained with the blood of four men.

Sága burst through a cluster of guards, sending them flying as she lashed her hands out. She arched her sword wildly, catching a guard under his faceplate. He fell with a pained grunt, and Sága kept going, grinning with deep satisfaction as the Warriors Three and Sif, in the distance, looked toward the scene with alarm. All around her, guards ran toward her, their weapons held high, reflecting the moonlight.

She was no more afraid of them than the breeze that cooled her cheeks.

Sága watched as Sif ran toward her, beckoning for the Warriors Three to follow. Sága was familiar with the formation: they'd been tasked with guarding the castle, of course, and Odin was smart to do so—he was aware that she wanted what was within. However, in this moment, even more, she wanted to feel the final beat of Sif's heart on the end of her blade.

Sága lifted her sword above her head as a swarm of guards rushed toward her from behind, letting out a wailing laugh as she and Sif ran at each other.

"It has been too long, Sif!" Sága shrieked. "Too long indeed!"

CHAPTER SEVEN

SHE KNOWS US

As they entered the barren lands, Thor peered over the side of the craft. Six bodies wearing the golden armor of Odin, bereft of life, lay on the dry, cracked ground, their blood seeping into the earth below.

"Your guards," Thor remarked. The edge was gone from his voice.

"It is what I feared," Odin murmured, but did not pause in flight. He turned toward a mountain that looked like bone jutting out of the barren earth in the moonlight, and prepared to dock.

Once they touched ground, Odin led Thor directly up the mountain.

"You've been here before, Father," Thor said, keeping pace with Odin, who seemed to know exactly where he was going.

"Aye."

"This is the mountain that Sif uncovered."

For a moment, Odin made no sound but the scrape of

his boots climbing up the mountain. After some time, he repeated the word again, this time more somberly. "Aye."

"Is it Sif who mistakenly unleashed this enemy of Asgard?" Thor asked. "If so, perhaps we should head back to fight alongside of her. What do you hope to find if you know for sure that this foe has been awakened?"

"I hope," Odin said, pulling himself up onto a plateau, "that I am mistaken. I hope that I find this chamber undisturbed. Because if I am right in my thought . . ."

Odin trailed off, his eyes distant as he reached down a hand to help Thor up. Thor wanted to urge him to continue, but knew that he'd pushed his father as far as he would go. Whatever secrets were hidden within the mountain, Thor suspected he would soon discover them firsthand.

They stood together on a flat surface of rock with a hole punched into the center—the cavern that Sif had described the night before. As Odin carefully descended into the pit, Thor stepped into the hole in the rock and dropped through nothingness. He landed on his feet with grace and power, sending a shudder through the mountain as his boots touched stone. He didn't wait for Odin, but instead took off down the spiraling path without so much as a glance over his shoulder. In the moments that followed, he heard his father's step catch up behind him, but did not turn to address the man.

The path, after some time, opened up into a platform

out of reach of the torches' glow. Odin's eyes darted around expectantly, his already grim expression darkening.

"May our ancestors protect us and Valhalla receive us," Odin murmured under his breath. He looked for a moment as if he was going to fall.

"What is it?" Thor asked.

Odin ignored him, and instead cast his gaze upward, as if speaking to a giant. "Hello!" he bellowed. "It is I, Odin, your creator and king! Address me and light my path!"

The silence hung heavily, as did the darkness.

Odin, cursing, reached into his armor and pulled out a small pouch of amber beads. He emptied the beads into his hand and, with a flick of his wrist, tossed them to the ground. They exploded on impact, and a golden, gaseous cloud raised from the shattered orbs, collecting in the air above them. The gas cast a dim light, but it was enough to see the wreckage.

What looked like an assembly of broken, melted Destroyers lined the platform. The enchanted suits of armor were twisted and discolored from whatever had burned them, their fragmented parts littering the ground beside a sarcophagus. There was also a shattered, black stone tablet, its thick pieces forming a semicircle around the casket.

"This reminds me of Midgard junkyards," Thor said, picking up the broken shell of a breastplate. "The humans keep their trash in heaping scraps, smashing them together into metallic cubes. What *is* all of this?"

Odin ignored Thor's question, and instead walked toward the broken pieces of black stone. He bent, visibly trembling, and picked up one of the chunks in his hand. He cupped the black shard in his palms as if holding something holy.

"Who is it that you kept prisoner down here, hidden from Asgard?" Thor asked. "Hidden from even your son, the future king?"

Odin turned to Thor, a grave expression on his face. "I did this *for* you, Son. For you and for Loki."

Thor, no longer able to contain his fury, strode past Odin and grabbed the lid of the sarcophagus. He felt it move under his hand, and knew that he would be able to rip it off with a single motion.

"You blamed *me* for this!" Thor snapped, casting his gaze down. "You thought I would unleash she who you kept in this tomb? I shall ask again: *who* is she?"

"You *cannot* know, my child," Odin said, standing. "You must fight her as a stranger, Thor, or you may find yourself unable to fight her at all."

"Will the secret to her identity be revealed in this casket?" Thor asked, digging his fingers under the lid.

"No," Odin said. "She is *gone*. There is nothing to learn here, Thor, but confirmation that the *worst* has happened. That we are at war."

Thor ripped the lid off of the sarcophagus and found

himself greeted with a familiar face, caked with blood and purple with bruises. The figure lay on a worn, plush cushion that lined the surface of the sarcophagus, stained and crusted with blood.

"Loki!" Thor cried, reaching in to pull his brother's still form from the casket. He reached his arms under Loki's back and lifted him up. He was limp, dead weight.

Cradling Loki, Thor lowered himself to the ground and laid his beaten brother on the stone floor before him.

Odin rose to his feet and approached, but Thor held out a hand, stopping him before he could take another step. Thor, his heart hammering under his armor, put his ear to Loki's chest, praying that he would hear his brother's heartbeat as well. Loki's head lolled on his shoulders, his black hair matted to his face, his eyes vacant.

"Brother, please," Thor murmured, frantically pulling off the thick, green and black hide that Loki used to armor his chest. "Please . . ."

"Does he live?" Odin asked, his voice pained.

Thor again pressed his ear to Loki's chest and, indeed, heard his brother's heart throb, weak and distant as a fading echo. The God of Thunder embraced his brother on the ground, relief flooding his chest as he held him. As Thor let go, Loki shuddered with a ragged cough. Thor propped him up against the sarcophagus and, wiping his eyes, took a step back. He grabbed his hammer again, knowing that this moment of peace, of which Loki was unaware, would be nothing but a memory as soon as the Trickster saw Thor.

Loki, looking especially gaunt under the golden light of Odin's cloud charm, let out a deep groan. He rolled his head slowly, cracking his neck with a sharp *pop*. With a sluggish wince, Loki opened his eyes and cast his gaze upward, his eyes settling on Thor.

"Found me," Loki rasped with a weak laugh.

"What have you done, Loki?" Odin bellowed from behind Thor, the sudden anger taking even the thunder god by surprise.

"Ohhhhhh, Thor," Loki said, continuing to chuckle as he pointed up at his brother. "Look at you. Loooook at you. You see it now, don't you? You see what I saw all that time ago?"

"And what would that be?" Thor asked, unable to look at his brother with the contempt his father mustered in that moment.

"You see the old man for what he is," Loki said, baring his teeth in a bloody grin. "You see it now."

"You, Loki, have damned us all!" Odin said. "Tell me, you miserable, cruel wretch, tell me what she said to you!"

Loki, unfazed by Odin's insults, grinned up at Thor. "Father did a wicked, wicked thing . . ."

Before either Thor or Odin could answer, the distant call of Asgard's war horns filled the air, reaching them even in the depths of the mountain. That specific sound, urgent and prolonged, could only mean one thing.

"She has breached the castle," Odin said through gritted teeth, stalking toward Loki with a hand ready to strike his son.

Thor caught Odin's hand before it could reach Loki, glaring at his beloved father with unrestrained ferocity. "Take him to safety."

"*Take* him? Thor, what do you—"

"Sif and the Warriors Three would *never* let this assailant past the gates if they drew breath," Thor said, ripping his hand away from Odin's. He pointed at his father with Mjolnir, his hand steady though his legs shook with fear. "Remember what I said."

"Thor—"

"REMEMBER!" Thor barked, and held Mjolnir toward the opening in the cavern far above, preparing to take off. Thunder boomed and lightning flashed in the sky above as Thor gathered his power.

"Sága!" Loki called out.

Thor looked at Loki under his shoulder as Mjolnir charged with electricity.

"Her name is Sága," Loki said, his smile fading. "And she . . . she *knows* us, Thor."

Thor shot out of the cavern with the speed of a lightning bolt, rocketing into the sky. He held his mighty hammer out in front of him as it guided his flight, headed straight for the capitol city of Asgard, not allowing himself to envision what horrors awaited him at home.

Sága, the mystical energy she'd stolen flowing through her veins, was a blur of motion even to her own eyes. She lashed out at Odin's guards all around her, dancing around their lashing sword strokes with ease and grace. Through the flurry of blades, she saw Volstagg pushing his way through.

She decided, then, that he would fall first.

Sága wrapped her hand around a guard's neck and kicked her legs up. Using the guard as a launching point, she spun around, feeling his neck snap in her grip, and flung herself toward Volstagg. She kicked out her feet, propelling herself into the warrior's bulbous stomach. Volstagg reeled back, but wasn't deterred. He righted himself and lifted his sword, charging at Sága once again.

Sága caught his blade with hers and saw, out of the corner of her eye, Hogun leaping over the piled bodies of fallen guards, moving toward them. Sága, less interested in seeing Hogun suffer than Volstagg, spun around and grabbed a guard by the face. She ripped off his helmet and delivered a crunching uppercut to his chin, sending him backward.

"Face me, coward!" Volstagg bellowed, swinging his sword at her again.

"That's the point," Sága growled, leaning her head to the side to dodge the blow. Without looking, she whipped her arm to the side, sending the guard's helmet toward Hogun. It blurred through the air as fast as Thor's lightning bolts and pegged Hogun in the forehead with a sick crack. Hogun fell forward, landing on the ground, facedown.

Sága smiled as she saw the color drain from Volstagg's pink face.

She slashed at him with her sword, and he parried her blows. He was ten times the warrior she remembered. When she knew him, he was a petty boy, prone to jokes and cruelty at Loki's expense. Though she smiled at his amusing stories and jokes when they were in a group, she remembered inwardly burning with anger when he made fun of those who weren't there to defend themselves.

It seemed that he had grown in the time since Sága last exchanged blows with him. But she didn't know the man he was, and wouldn't mourn him when he fell.

Ready to end it, Sága grasped her swords with both hands, reached into the well of mystical energy she stored deep within her power center, and swung with all of her might at Volstagg's sword. The blade flew out of the voluminous warrior's hands, clattering to the side.

"*VOLSTAGG!*" Fandral called from the distance. With Sif

by his side, he ran toward Sága, but she wasn't worried. She had spread this fight out in Odin's courtyard not to section the Warriors Three off strategically, but because it was *fun* to watch them scramble.

Sága punched Volstagg in the chest, feeling a satisfying crack. She followed through with another punch, and another. Volstagg fell to his knees before her, and she pointed her sword at his neck.

"*NO! VOLSTAGG!*" Sif screamed. She was getting close.

"Who are you?" Volstagg croaked, looking up at Sága not in desperation, but pure confusion.

When Loki didn't recognize her, even though she knew he wouldn't, it hurt. With Volstagg, it nearly made her break into a fit of laughter.

Instead, she just smiled. "It doesn't matter. Not to you."

Sága pulled back one of her swords and, as Sif's and Fandral's screams built in the background, slammed the hilt into Volstagg's temple. The warrior instantly fell unconscious, hitting the ground with a painful thud.

Sága spun around in time to catch dual blows from Fandral and Sif on her sword. She pulled back, moving with incredible speed as Fandral aimed his sword lower, at her vital organs, while Sif swung high.

"You make a beautiful team," Sága shouted over the music of the swords clashing. "If only Odin's guards fought with such skill and unity, perhaps they'd be alive. How odd that your king doesn't choose the most skilled warriors to act as his iron fist. Could it be that he doesn't trust those strong enough to think and act on their own?"

"Shut your mouth!" Fandral barked, jabbing at her with the sword. Even with her mystically enhanced speed, he nicked her hip. "What do you know of the All-Father?"

"An answer in the form of a question," Sága said. "Do you know my name?"

"You are an enemy of Asgard," Fandral said. "You have no name to me."

"As I thought," Sága said. She whipped her swords around and ducked low, cutting through Sif's calf. As Sif fell, Sága dipped backward to avoid a wild thrust from Fandral and then sliced downward, cutting Fandral's shoulder.

Fandral twisted in pain, but held on to the blade. Sága kicked Sif aside, and, dropping one of her swords, grabbed Fandral by his wounded shoulder, digging her thumb into the cut. She pressed until, finally, Fandral's blade dropped next to her own.

"If you don't know my name, then I promise you, Fandral, I know Odin like you never will," Sága said. She shot her head forward, cracking her skull into Fandral's. Like Volstagg and Hogun before him, he dropped.

Sága stepped over the fallen form of Fandral and moved toward Sif, who stumbled backward over her bleeding leg. Sif righted herself and, face set in a fierce scowl, held her blade with both hands, preparing for Sága's next onslaught.

"The silent warrior," Sága said. "Lady Sif, you have no words for your old friend?"

Sif glared at Sága. For a moment, Sága thought that Sif might not respond at all, that she had grown into a hardened, emotionless assassin like so many of the other Asgardians who had been raised as warriors.

"How?" Sif asked at last as Odin's war horns cut through the night. "The Warriors Three are legend. Who are you that . . . that they fall to your blade? That *all* of Odin's guard lie at our feet, dead?"

Sága looked past Sif, into the open doors leading into Odin's palace.

"I know you, Sif," Sága said. "You wish to delay me, so that Thor might return before I can walk through those doors."

"*How?*" Sif repeated. "You wanted me to speak—I'm speaking. How?"

Sága grinned, her eyes flashing with all colors of the rainbow. She rolled her shoulders, feeling the stolen mystical power coursing through her veins. With the energy of the seven Destroyer guards as well as the once glorious Rainbow Bridge residing in her power center, she knew she could grab Sif and burn the soul out of her with little effort. That would be a waste of her power, though—and she had such beautiful plans.

"It won't matter if Thor arrives, old friend," Sága said,

taking a great leap toward Sif. She extended her boot and slammed it into Sif's chest, sending her flying backward, crashing through the barricaded doors and into Odin's hall. The golden beams that held the doors cracked as the doors fell to rubble from the sudden, vicious blow. Sága landed in front of the ruined doors, cracking the tile below her and, leaving the prostrate forms of the Warriors Three and countless armored guards behind her, crossed the threshold into Odin's throne room.

Sif sprang back up and, letting out a battle cry, charged Sága. Sága met the stroke of Sif's sword with her arm, sending the sword flying across the room. Sif slammed her forehead into Sága's mouth, knocking the attacker's head back. Sága, her mouth filling with bitter blood, looked at Sif with a smirk.

"Impressive," Sága said. "You've become every bit the warrior you hoped to be. Too bad you will be Forgotten."

She slammed her knee into Sif's stomach and, before the raven-haired warrior could react, extended her leg for yet another devastating kick into Sif's chest. Sif hit the floor hard, rolling back toward Odin's throne. Sága threw herself into the air, landing with crushing weight on Sif's chest. Sága dug her knees into her old friend's sternum, her eyes widening with delight as Sif, ever the fighter, peppered Sága's sides with a flurry of punches, even as the towering, wicked Asgardian crushed the air out of her lungs.

Sága grabbed Sif by the throat, digging her fingers into the back of the warrior's neck. With a single twist, the Lady Sif would be no more—but that wasn't what Sága wanted. The guards could perish, but she had a much nastier fate in mind for those she once called her friends. It's why the Warriors Three, though incapacitated, still lived. But perhaps Sif, as strong as she was, and as much as Sága had missed her, deserved a quicker end. Maybe she deserved that mercy.

Sága tightened her grip on Sif's neck, looking down at her friend with a softening gaze. "I hope, in the halls of Valhalla, you remember me as I will choose to remember you, and you alone. My name was Sága, and we were friends. I loved you. And now, I will mourn you."

"Release her."

The command came from behind Sága, powerful and clear. Sága knew its speaker well. She peered over her shoulder to see her one-time queen, Frigga, holding a dazzling silver blade to her, right below the ear.

"Frigga," Sága said. "It has been—"

"You are to address me as 'my queen,' Sága," Frigga commanded. "And you are to obey me. Release Sif."

Sága looked down at Sif, who was beginning to lose consciousness in her grasp. With a smile, Sága opened her hand, letting Sif's head hit the floor. She withdrew her knee from Sif's chest and stood to her full height, looking down on Frigga.

"You know me," Sága said.

"Odin's spells may work on most," Frigga said. "But not the queen of Asgard. I remember you well, Sága. The good and the bad. I thought, for some time, that you were a dream. You haunted my resting hours. Since discovering the truth, I think of you often."

"And I think of *you* often as well," Sága said. "Of your betrayal."

"What of yours?" Frigga asked, training the point of the sword on Sága's neck.

"Just recompense for unjust punishment," Sága snarled. "Much like what you see before you."

"You believe this crusade of yours to be justified," Frigga said. "Asgard bleeds. Those who once spoke your name with love lie dying. Where is the justice in that?"

"I am not here to kill those who forget my name," Sága said, resting her eyes on the blade of Frigga's sword.

"What, then?" Frigga snapped.

Sága lashed out her fist with such speed that her arm was a blur to her own eyes. The silver sword shattered into fragments upon impact, leaving the stunned queen holding a hilt with nothing but a shard of blade feebly pointing toward Sága.

"You can stand in my path and, before you can blink, I will present you with the Lady Sif's head!" Sága shouted, snatching the hilt from Frigga's hands. She flung it across the room toward Odin's throne, where it lodged in the cushion where the All-Father's head would be were he sitting there. "Or you can remove her *and* yourself from sight."

"Thor is coming," Frigga said, positioning herself between Sága and Sif, who was already trying to get up, despite her injuries. "I don't know whose powers you have drained to gain such strength so quickly, but there is no amount of magic you can absorb that would make you my son's equal."

Sága walked by Frigga, who remained by Sif's side. In the distance, beyond the throne, was a golden hall protected by, Sága knew, the Destroyer. That old thing did not concern her. Once it fell, there would be nothing stopping her from entering into Odin's vault, where he kept all manner of mystically enchanted weapons. Once she was there, there was no power in any of the realms, Asgard or beyond, that would stop her.

CHAPTER EIGHT
RAINBOW'S END

Lightning cracked through the black night skies of Asgard as Thor rocketed through the air, his hammer pointed at his father's fortress. He swung the great Mjolnir downward and shot down, a burst of electricity surging out behind him. Thunder could be heard in all corners of the Realm Eternal as Thor landed at the gates leading to the throne room, where the lifeless bodies of Odin's guards were strewn about, broken and silent.

Thor's eyes washed over the scene, searching for his friends. He saw Hogun first, laid out on the ground, moaning lowly as he reached out to Thor. He was by his friend's side instantly, holding Hogun's hand. The great warrior was bruised nearly beyond recognition, his face caked with blood from a gash in his forehead, his features distorted with swelling.

"S-Sif . . ." Hogun choked out.

Thor looked over at Volstagg and Fandral laying off to the side, defeated and still. Volstagg's great belly slowly rose and fell with breath, though, and Fandral's fingers twitched.

Thor looked down to Hogun, his mind racing. "Can you speak, friend?"

"Yes," Hogan croaked. "Thor, you must . . ." He winced, clearly dazed.

"Tell me Hogun, why would an assailant who made sure to slay Odin's guards leave the Warriors Three, mightier foes by any estimation, alive?" Thor asked. "Who is this woman?"

"Sif . . ." Hogun said.

"Sif?" Thor asked. "My friend, you're not thinking straight—"

"No. In-inside," Hogun sputtered. "*Sif.* She is alone with this devil. Sh-she's beyond our power, Thor. Something is wrong. . . . She is . . . she is more than a god."

Thor propped Hogun against the golden railing leading up the ramp to the castle's doors. "I shall return, my friend. We will, all of us, live to fight another day."

With those words, Thor was off, bursting into the throne room just in time to see Frigga with her arm around an injured Sif, helping the limping warrior toward the hall.

"Mother," Thor called, running to her. He marked the shards that had been Frigga's sword on the floor, and felt his blood boil as he imagined what had happened here, before his father's throne.

Frigga turned to Thor with a severity in her eyes that he had scarcely seen in all of his life. Sif leaned on the queen, in a state similar to Hogun—alive, but barely. Her armor was cracked and dented—she had been hit by both blade and immense blunt force.

"Sif," Thor started, "Mother, will she sur—"

"Your father's vault," Frigga interrupted, spitting out the words as quickly as she could. "Go—now!"

Knowing from his mother's tone that he had no time to waste or ask why, Thor spun around and raced toward the vault. Past the throne, down a winding, labyrinthine series of halls, and toward a set of doors almost as thick as the span of Thor's arms, he burst into the entrance to the vault only to be greeted with a chilling sight.

The Destroyer, his father's bewitched suit of armor designed to protect the vault, lay broken, scattered before him. Thor, who had himself fought the Destroyer on many occasions, couldn't believe his eyes. Who was this warrior that could slay the royal guards of Asgard, defeat the Warriors Three and the unshakable Lady Sif, and break the Destroyer as if it were a child's toy?

Thor looked past the broken armor and toward the center of the vault, where Odin's treasures and magical oddities were stored. In the middle of the heaping riches, a silhouetted figure stared at him from the distance, its head cocked to the side.

Thor grasped Mjolnir, holding his trusted hammer at the ready.

The figure stepped forward, into the light. Thor glared at her, his knuckles white. Roped, blonde hair, matted with blood and sweat. Scars lining muscles, wounds both new and old. A vicious grin spread across her dry, cracked lips as she pointed one of Odin's treasured swords at Thor. A purple aura shimmered with mystical power. Eyes glimmered with rainbow light.

"Who are you?" Thor asked, his mind racing as he remembered his mother's words. *I thought she was a dream.*

"*You* are Thor," she said. "Who am I, Odinson?"

Thor clenched his teeth. Had he never dreamed of this woman? Suddenly, he felt dizzy looking upon her. Dreams of childhood anxieties, of forgetting to go to his sword-fighting lessons, forgetting to wear clothing out in public, forgetting to attend his coronation as king of Asgard; all of these silly, laughable boyhood nightmares of forgetting something important, something essential to who he was, overcame him.

Sága stared at him, waiting patiently, with a calm, knowing grin.

"Sága," Thor said. "You are Sága."

She stopped in her tracks, the rainbow lights faded from her eyes, revealing milky white pupils. The rigidity of her posture eased as she looked at Thor, squinting at him in disbelief.

"You remember?" she asked.

Thor, fighting through the strange feeling, took a step toward Sága, keeping his hammer at the ready. "You spoke your name to my brother before beating him with no mercy, leaving him for dead in a casket hidden in the bowels of a mountain," Thor bellowed. "For the little time I have known your name, I know that when it is spoken, terror and pain follow."

Sága narrowed her eyes, letting out a guttural curse as she took another step toward Thor. "Of course. Of *course*."

"What do you hope to gain from this attack?" Thor charged. He gestured toward the heaping coin behind her. "Riches? You mean to cart this gold out of here handful by handful?"

"No," Sága said. "I already have what I want."

"And what is that?" Thor asked.

In a blur of motion, Sága was in front of Thor. Before he could even lift a hand to react, he felt a splitting pain in his face and a burst of dazzling rainbow light. He fell back, blood flowing from his nose as Sága looked down at him.

"All of the mystical power that Odin has hidden over all of the years," she said, waving her hands at Thor. They sparkled with glowing, violet energy. "Everything I needed to pass final judgment upon Asgard."

Thor kicked his feet up, landing in standing position behind Sága. He swung Mjolnir at the back of Sága's head, but she was too fast. She leaned forward, avoiding the blow, and spun around, aiming a kick at Thor's throat. This time, Thor was ready. He ducked the kick and charged Sága, scooping her outstretched leg up in one hand and grabbing her arm with the other. He slammed her into the wall of the vault, using the weight of his own body to overpower her.

Unfazed from the blow, Sága kicked her other leg up and bashed her knee into Thor's ear, sending the God of Thunder stumbling away from her and into a pile of coins. Kicking them aside, Thor wound Mjolnir up until it, too, was a blur and then, just as Sága was about to rush him, let the great hammer fly.

Sága dodged the strike but Mjolnir clipped her shoulder. Running quickly, Thor delivered a powerful punch to her stomach as Mjolnir returned to his other outstretched hand. He swung it down to connect with her collarbone, and then up again to crack into her chin. Invigorated by the series of blows, he reeled back Mjolnir to deliver the knockout blow, a sharp and decisive strike to Sága's chest when the mysterious assailant caught Thor's arm in her grasp.

She twisted sharply to the side, and Thor thought for a moment that she'd ripped his forearm in two. Pain drove down Thor's arm as Mjolnir fell from his hand and landed with a booming thud on the floor.

"Say you remember me," Sága hissed. "*SAY IT!*"

Sága dug her fingers deeper into his arm, and the mighty Asgardian bellowed. He grabbed at her, trying to get her off of him, but she dug deeper and deeper with her iron grasp.

"I loved you," Sága said. "I loved you as a brother."

Shaking, Thor held out his other hand, and Mjolnir zoomed across the room, smacking into his palm. He swung for Sága, but she released him and leapt backward. The hammer struck nothing but air.

Thor stood, breathing heavily as blood flowed down his mangled forearm.

"Who are you?" he asked again. "I don't know you. This . . . this is *madness*."

Sága nodded. "I concur, old friend."

With a burst of rainbow light, bringing to Thor's mind an image of the Bifrost's glow on a dark, starless night, Sága was gone.

Thor, his arm numbing from the pain, didn't waste any time recuperating. He burst out of the vault, shot through the throne room, and raced into Odin's yard. As he ran, he saw Frigga once again, though this time the Lady Sif was not with her. Frigga turned to Thor, a panicked shine in her eyes.

"She's gone," Frigga said. "Before I could stop her, she *left*."

"I know," Thor said, looking out at the dark forest before her, hoping against all logic that he'd spot Sága. "Her speed is greater than anything I've ever seen. She has somehow gathered incredible mystical power—but it's *stolen* power.

If we can reduce her to her natural state, we can best her in combat and then—"

"Thor, no," Frigga said. "*Sif.* She ran away when I was attempting to nurse her wounds. She chased Sága into the woods."

Thor snarled and pointed his hammer up, ready to take to the sky. Frigga touched his shoulder, staying him for a moment.

"She was once one of us, Thor," Frigga said. "She . . . I-I'm so sorry, my Son. I'm so, so sorry."

Thor furrowed his brow, studying his mother's watery eyes. "I don't understand. But when Sif is safe," Thor growled, "you will tell me *everything.*"

"I would that I had earlier. Your father believed silence was best for us all, and I agreed at the time. If only we knew."

"Where did they go?" Thor asked. "Did you see?"

Frigga shook her head. "I didn't."

Thor gestured with his injured arm to the Warriors Three, who had now gathered together against the railing. "Take care of them. I know not why Sága has kept them alive while slaughtering the guard, but . . ."

Thor trailed off, narrowing his eyes.

"What is it, Son?"

"She didn't kill them, or me, or Sif, or you," Thor said. "Not even Loki. And you said she was one of *us*. She called me her old friend."

"Yes," Frigga said with a solemn nod. "She was."

"And yet, she says that she will pass final judgment upon Asgard," Thor said. "I know exactly where she's gone! The Bifrost!"

He heard his mother shout after him, but he did not answer. He burst into the sky as lighting flashed and thunder boomed, headed for the Rainbow Bridge.

Thor landed on the Rainbow Bridge, but it looked nothing like the Bifrost he'd traveled upon his whole life. Its colors and radiance was gone. Thor looked down upon a barren icicle, empty of light and life. At the end of the dead Bifrost, at the threshold of the observatory entrance, Sága stood over Heimdall's limp form. Her body glowed with a shifting aura of purple, golden, and—rainbow, all of the colors, light and crystalline, dancing together.

"You," Thor growled, swinging his hammer as he raced toward her. The Rainbow Bridge, now brittle, let out a sharp splintering sound every time his foot landed on it. Gaseous magical energy, its once brilliant color faded, leaked from the cracks. Thor pointed Mjolnir at Sága. "*You did this!*"

Sága stepped over Heimdall and looked at Thor with violent ferocity. "Did you intend to go somewhere, brave warrior? Exalted son of Asgard, future king of *nothing*?"

"I realized that you would attempted to destroy the

Bifrost," Thor screamed, lighting gathering on his hammer as he threw himself into the air for a great leap, arching toward Sága. "You attempt to pass some kind of judgment on all of Asgard for whatever perceived wrongs have been committed against you. Of course you would prevent any escape!"

He swung the hammer forward and sent a mighty bolt of electricity down at Sága. She held out her hands as if to catch the lighting, and instead of striking her down, it flowed into her hands, palms drinking the power up.

"Wrong, Thor. I drained the Bifrost before my assault on the fortress," Sága said. "I came here to collect Heimdall, now that the trials begin."

Thor landed on the Bifrost, wincing as its frail surface splintered like ice under his feet. "There will be no trials. Whatever insanity you wish to visit upon this realm, know this. I will not stand idly by. I will fight you at every turn, defending Asgard, until my heart beats no more."

Sága stared at Thor, an almost tranquil air about her distant gaze. "I know."

In a flash of blinding power that crackled off of her rigid form, Sága was upon Thor. She slammed him into the brittle Bifrost, which cracked deeply with the impact. Her palms glowed with bright rainbow light as she strangled Thor.

"I wonder," she said. The concentrated power of the Bifrost, collected in her palm, scalded Thor's neck. He knew if he didn't get away from her, it would kill him in only moments. "If I strike you, Thor, with the full power of the Rainbow Bridge, will you burn to ash? Or will you be cast out into the nothingness of space? It isn't quite what I had in mind for you, I admit, but there is a certain poetry to it."

"Sága," Thor rasped, pulling at her hands. "If you truly were one of us, if you know us and loved us as you say you did, you can—"

"Hah!" she laughed, a joyless, cruel sound. "If you knew the truth, you'd think that's hilarious."

A voice came from behind them, at the other end of the bridge. "I know the truth!"

"SIF!" Thor yelled. "Stay back!"

Sága, grinning, threw herself off Thor, her aura of rainbow power a mystical flame floating up into the air. Suspended above the powerless Bifrost, she looked down at Thor and Sif with a sneer.

Sif ran to Thor's side as the God of Thunder stood, ready to fight again.

"I came to stop her," Sif said, her eyes wild. "Frigga told me everything about Sága. Listen to me, Thor—she's never going to give in to words. She will not listen to anything we say."

"Tell him why!" Sága barked from the skies, holding out a hand toward Thor and Sif like a vindictive god preparing to smite them.

"She was our friend," Sif said, her breath ragged. Thor could see that despite her grievous injuries, she'd run from the castle all the way to the Rainbow Bridge, and had only arrived a few moments short of Thor, who had used the power of Mjolnir to fly there. "We fought against her rather than save her. And then, we forgot her. We let Odin hide her away in a tomb, her own memory intact, while she was erased from our history and our minds."

Thor shook his head, looking from Sif to Sága. "I don't understand. If she was truly our friend as you said, we would never do this. It isn't the Asgardian way. It isn't my way."

Sága scowled, her face a mask of pure hatred as she stared down at Thor and Sif. "And yet."

Sif held her blade at the ready and Thor grasped Mjolnir. They stood shoulder to shoulder, looking up at Sága.

"Together," Thor said.

"Aye," Sif replied, her body tensing as she prepared to spring into attack.

"Together it shall be, then!" Sága shrieked, and held out her hand. A lightning bolt burst from her palm and rocketed toward Thor and Sif. The Asgardian warriors spun around and raced away, but as the blast came toward them, it expanded in size.

Thor held out Mjolnir and grabbed Sif's hand, taking flight with his friend in tow. They lifted off the dead Rainbow Bridge as Sága's combined attack of stolen energies—Thor's lightning and the sacred power of the Bifrost—obliterated the glassy surface under them. The impact spread like a crashing wave, sending the energy surging toward Thor and Sif, far faster than Thor was flying.

As the roar of the energy became deafening, Thor watched in horror as the wave of rainbow power raced toward them, far too quick to escape. Sif looked at him with a blank stare and held on to his hand as Thor's vision filled with the pulsing, scalding energy of the Bifrost. As he and Sif were caught in the explosion, he tried to call out to her, "HOLD ON!"

Thor couldn't even hear himself. All he could hear above the overwhelming rush of exploding magical energy was Sága's distant, barking laugh.

Sága stood at the end of a crystal cliff. The Rainbow Bridge was decimated, and both Thor and Sif were gone. Sága had now expended much of the power that she'd absorbed from the enchanted armor guarding her sarcophagus, the Bifrost, the Destroyer, and Odin's treasures to do so, but it had been worth it.

And there was always more power to steal in Asgard for those who knew where to find it.

Sága turned around, striding over to Heimdall. She knelt, scooping the great watcher of Asgard up in her arms, and threw him over her shoulder.

"The time has come, Heimdall," she said as she took flight, suspended in the air by her stolen powers. She had sufficient power left to fly back to the castle, and certainly enough to dispense with Odin when he returned—a reunion she'd cherish above all others.

She spoke to Heimdall, knowing that he could not hear her words, but finding that even an unconscious ear was better than the perfect darkness of her sarcophagus.

"You've seen so much, my wise old friend," she said. "I remember sitting with you on the Rainbow Bridge, and you'd tell me such beautiful stories. No one knew Asgard like you."

She sighed deeply as the kingdom came into view below.

"And soon Asgard will not know *you* at all."

CHAPTER NINE

REMEMBER

He stood before the pond in his yard, laughing at his rippling reflection. On his left was Sif, her arm linked with his. On his right, was Sága, her cheeks red from laughter as she threw stones into the water. When her hand was empty, she knelt down to the grass and pulled two more stones from the dirt, and chucked them into the water, aiming for the head of Thor's reflection.

The stone pierced the water and Thor threw himself to the ground, acting as if he'd been struck in the temple. He laughed from the grass as Sága chased Sif around the pond, the taller Asgardian's blonde hair stretching behind her in a shock of braids as bright as armor. Sága, her aim precise, let the stone fly. It hit the water where Sif's face reflected back, laughing, but then skipped on the surface.

Sif pointed at Sága with a laugh. "Doesn't count!"

"Does too," Sága laughed, plopping down next to Thor. "What say you, Thor?"

Thor look from Sága to Sif, knowing that he was in trouble

no matter whose side he took. "I wasn't paying attention!" he fibbed, winking at Sága as Sif snorted.

"Hey, Thor . . ." Sága said, pulling a blade of grass from the ground. She had a distant look to her eyes, as if she was suddenly contemplating something beyond Thor's understanding. Thor had heard the elders speaking about her, how she, even as a girl of only thirteen, was wise for her years. Thor had taken umbrage with this, as he'd never walked in on a group of warriors saying that about him.

"Yes?" Thor said.

"Why does Loki so rarely emerge from his quarters?" Sága asked. "I miss him."

"You miss Loki!" Thor cried, and let out a cracking laugh. How he hated the way his voice cracked. To play it off, he puffed out his chest and took on a dismissive air, which he imagined must have looked quite impressive to Sága and Sif. "You may be the only one. Loki has taken to feeling sorry for himself despite being offered chance after chance to prove his worth. Alas, I do believe my brother is hopeless."

"Tell him to join us tomorrow," Sága said, looking at Thor with a sad smile. "Tell him I asked for him."

"Why?" Thor snorted.

Sif leaned down to Thor and punched him in the shoulder. Thor looked up at her with a scowl. "Hey!"

"Just tell him," Sif said, her brows raised. "Sága wants to see Loki. Everything isn't always about you, Thor."

"I-I know," Thor stuttered. "I shall tell him. But I warn you—should he fail to bathe, you may consider yourself fairly warned!"

Sága smiled again, though it did not reach her eyes. Thor followed her gaze toward the water, now still, which again reflected the three of them back. Thor couldn't help but grin at the image. He sighed, happy, and told himself silently that these may just be the best days of his life.

Thor's eyes snapped open to total, spinning blackness. Before he saw anything, he heard Sif scream.

"THOR!"

Thor's reverie broken, he grew dizzy as the stars swirled around him, rainbow energy bursting past in arcs of color. Below him, hanging on to his forearm, was Sif. The exploding Bifrost was reflected in her eyes as they careened through space and, for one peaceful moment, Thor thought that, as far as final visions go, beautiful Sif with her gleaming eyes was a fine one indeed.

"THOR!" Sif pulled Thor toward her with a powerful tug. They whipped wildly through the shattered Bifrost, scalding hot explosions going off in all directions, adding a flash of color to the blackness of space. Now clinging to his shoulder, Sif pointed one arm ahead.

Thor looked at her, wondering if the explosion had driven her mad.

"Can you hear me?!" Sif hissed.

"Yes!" Thor replied.

"Then we're *not* yet among the stars!" Sif cried. She pointed ahead, toward a brilliant flash of Bifrost energy. "The Rainbow Bridge is fractured—but we're still inside its energy. Use your hammer!"

Thor narrowed his eyes, confused as to her meaning until yet another burst of rainbow light filled his vision to the left. With a smirk spreading over his face, Thor spun Mjolnir until it became a blur of silver and blue energy crackling at the end of his arm. He extended his arm left, grasping the hammer as tightly as he could, and rocketed toward the core of the Bifrost explosion. He thought desperately of his second home—the realm where he had become an Avenger, where his friends lived and fought, where he had become known as a god. The realm that, when he perished, brought him back to life with their beliefs. The realm he fought for and that he vowed to, should war arise, die for.

Midgard. Earth.

With Sif grasping his side, bracing herself for the impact, Thor shot through the combusting cloud. He felt intense relief overcome him, as if he'd jumped into a bath of scalding water—and then, in a flash, everything went white.

• • •

Thor sat cross legged in the field with Volstagg, doubled over laughing as his friend lifted his shirt up and folded his voluminous belly over to form a mouth. He made the flaps of his stomach slap against each other and, in an exaggerated falsetto, imitated Loki, whose voice was just now beginning to crack.

"I am Loki, son of Odin!" Volstagg piped, moving his stomach about with each word. "By the mighty crack of my voice, delicate as it may be, I will defend Asgard until I fall! Which, if we were attacked and I was in charge, I'd wager would be almost instantly! However, I . . ."

Volstagg trailed off, looking past Thor with an inquisitive gaze. Thor turned to see Sága, her arms folded protectively across her chest, striding toward them with a hurried step.

Thor stood. "What vexes you, Sága?"

She came to a stop, her blonde braids rolling over her arms as she looked both ways. She opened her mouth to talk, and then looked at Volstagg.

"I must talk to Thor," she said, "in private."

Volstagg chuckled, the obliviousness clear on his round and shiny face. "Well have at it!" he said.

Thor smacked him in the arm, his eyes widening with urgency. Tension poured off Sága and he knew whatever she had to say was serious. "Leave, friend."

"Oh!" Volstagg said with mock reverence. He bowed to Sága. "She humbly requests an audience with the future king

of Asgard. Bow before Thor and kiss his ring while I, Volstagg, peasant son of peasants, scurry off like a fleck of unwanted dust caught in the breezes of—"

Thor moved to shove Volstagg, who ran away with a chuckle. Sága watched him disappear down the hill and then turned to Thor with a frosty gaze in her eyes.

"You mock your brother openly," she said.

"I do not," Thor said, crinkling his brow. "Volstagg was just having some fun."

"At Loki's expense."

"Yet you criticize me, while you perch unseen like a raven, listening to words not meant for your ears," Thor snapped. Sága's cold stare didn't falter at the stern retort, and Thor instantly felt bad. Sága remained one of his closest friends, even as she grew closer to Loki, who seemed more and more distant from Thor over the passing months. Thor, his voice softer, asked, "This is your urgent matter?"

"No."

Thor waited, but Sága cast her gaze downward, her teeth clenched as she stared down at her toes. Unnerved by the normally bold girl's solemnity, Thor pressed on. "What is it, Sága?"

"I feel wicked for sharing this with you, Thor," she replied. "Doing so will be breaking words shared in confidence."

Thor narrowed his eyes. "Loki."

Sága breathed in sharply, but didn't reply. She stood on the grassy hill, the majestic Kingdom of Asgard spreading out behind her in the distance. From Thor's vantage point, she looked like a giant.

"Is Loki . . . safe?" Thor asked. "Did something happen?"

Sága shook her head. "No. Nothing. It isn't Loki that is in danger. But I . . ."

"Please," he said. He put a hand on her back, trying to be as comforting as he could. He felt her shuddering at his touch, before a sob burst from her mouth. Startled, Thor peered at her face, watching fat tears cascade down her cheeks.

"He has been working on a bit of nasty sorcery that I believe may prove to be perilous," she said, hesitant. "He has created a small, clay figure onto which he plans to project an illusion. When he unleashes it in the kingdom, it will appear as a twenty-foot troll."

Thor couldn't hold back his chortle. Sága looked at him, plainly hurt. With an apologetic smile, Thor held up his hands in mock surrender.

"I'm sorry," Thor said. "I laugh not at you, but at Loki's idea."

"I do not find it funny at all," Sága retorted.

"Why does this scheme trouble you?" Thor asked. "You and I both know that Loki has been obsessed with his tricks recently."

"He means to put on this show of power to demonstrate to your father that his power is just as great as yours," Sága said. "He feels as if you are the favored son and that, as you grow toward adulthood, that Odin's favor grows with you. He means to impress them, Thor, but with such an illusion—I feel it to be dangerous. Reckless. What if, before Loki reveals the trick, something bad happens in pursuit of the troll?"

Thor smiled, relieved. He looked Sága in the eye, and spoke to her the way he'd imagine he'd do so if he were king. "All will be well, Sága. Loki means no harm . . . well, no real harm. This scheme is exactly that—an innocent scheme. I'm certain that everything will be okay."

Sága furrowed her brow. "What should we do?"

"Nothing," Thor said, with a shrug. "Perhaps we should watch? I'd like to see just how advanced my little brother's trickery has become."

"Are you sure?" Sága asked. "I know that, for matters of Asgardian safety, I'm meant to approach Odin, but I didn't want to risk getting Loki in trouble. I fear it would ruin the friendship we've built, and I could scarcely take that, Thor."

"I'm sure," Thor said. "You say 'friendship,' Sága, but the way Sif tells it, it appears that you and Loki may have a greater bond than that."

"And you say that I eavesdrop like the crow," Sága said, smiling for the first time in the conversation. "Loki is dear to me. I can only hope that, even though I've broken the bond of my promise to him, he considers me such as well."

"He'll never know," Thor said. "Come. Let's see what tricks he's got up his sleeve."

The two of them walked toward the Kingdom of Asgard, and Thor attempted to picture how the illusionary troll would attack. He chuckled at the thought. Nothing, though, not his imagination and not Sága's warning, could prepare him for what lay in wait at the castle.

It was this night that everything would change.

Thor woke again to blackness. Wind, brisk and soothing, whipped across his burned skin as he shot through the air. Devastation blossomed within his core as it dawned on him that Sif's idea hadn't worked—now, he was in an even deeper blackness with no stars and no explosions of Bifrost energy. He felt Sif holding on to him, but he no longer felt in control of his descent. Were they in some kind of afterlife dimension? Some dark, empty abyss for those who die while caught in the Bifrost?

Or . . .

His senses were flooded with familiar smells—halal food, smoke, garbage, coffee, and . . . asphalt. White spots dotted Thor's vision as his eyes, blinded temporarily from the scorching Bifrost explosion, regained their sight.

"Sif!" Thor said, laughing out loud. "I think we made it! The bridge took us back to the last place it accessed! New—"

Thor's vision cleared as pavement raced toward him from mere feet away, too close for even the God of Thunder to redirect. With a burst of rock and a grinding feeling digging into his already battered skull, Thor and Sif had landed in a pile of rubble that was, moments prior, the sidewalk of the Avenger's pizzeria of choice in Brooklyn. People gathered around the two fallen Asgardian warriors, murmuring and taking pictures, but all Thor could do was emit a long groan before he, once again, faded . . .

"You KNEW?!" Odin roared, his voice echoing through the cavernous throne hall. Somehow, each echo seemed angrier than the last.

Thor kneeled at his father's throne, his eyes wide as he looked up at Odin, who had never looked more like the god those from Midgard thought him to be. Wrathful and larger than life, Odin lowered his face to Thor's level, his eyes wide and his lips trembling.

"You stand before me, Thor, as the future king of Asgard, and profess that you knew of Loki's trickery in advance of tonight's gathering?" Odin questioned. He didn't wait for an answer. "In pursuit of this troll, this mockery of my kingdom and the reason we as Asgardians fight, two of my men lay dead."

Thor closed his eyes, feeling the guilt fresh again as the memory replayed. He'd watched it happen with his own eyes with Sága, sharing a knowing laugh as the guards prepared to attack the bewitched toy. Believing it to be a towering troll, two of Odin's guards had climbed to the fourth floor of the palace and leapt toward the troll's neck. However, as they did so, Loki's spell faltered and the magic that made the vision corporeal dissipated. The guards fell for what seemed to Thor like ages before landing. One of them landed on his neck, and the other fell upon another guard, whose blade pierced the fallen warrior's armor.

Loki had been dragged off for punishment that Thor was certain was as grave as it was earned. It took two sleepless nights of horrific dreams for Thor to approach Odin and confess that he'd known of Loki's plan and had dismissed it. He hadn't spoken a word to Sága, and couldn't even meet her eyes. What stung worse was that she had tried to stop Loki's plan and, instead of acting, Thor had spoken to her with what he thought was the advice of a calm, level-headed king. He'd never felt more the fool than this day.

"I am at fault," Thor said, his voice thick. "I take full responsibility."

"Did you think this would be amusing?" Odin barked. "Unlike Loki, you have taken all of the training courses offered by the finest swordsmen in Asgard. You know how dangerous battle can be, and yet you still conspire with your brother to commit these base acts of foolishness?"

"No, Father," Thor said. "It wasn't my plan. I was made aware of it, and failed to act. I would never—I didn't—"

"Hold your tongue," Odin said, circling Thor like a vulture. "You were 'made aware' of this plan, boy? Loki himself spoke these words to you?"

Thor cleared his throat. "I—"

"ANSWER ME!"

Thor looked up at Odin, whose chest rose and fell with rage. He could hardly believe that this was the man who had given him life, who had loved him so. He spoke to Thor as he spoke to an enemy of Asgard, and Thor despaired to know that this tone was well earned. How could he ever forgive himself for his part in this tragedy?

Odin knelt to Thor, lowering his voice to a harsh whisper. "You truly regret the blood shed in these halls over this reckless, cruel trick?"

Thor nodded. At almost seventeen years old, it had been a long time since he'd felt so much like a child.

"Tell me, then," Odin said, his tone hushed. "Tell me how you were made aware of Loki's plan."

Thor stared his father in the eye, his mind racing. He closed his eyes and thought back to days before on the hills, standing with Sága. He pictured himself acting as soon as she revealed Loki's scheme, taking off with her to inform Odin. Loki would protest and rage at him, and Sága as well, but it would be better than . . .

Thor winced as his mind was once again filled with the horrific memory of the two guards falling. He heard the sounds *every time, as if it were happening right here again. A sickening crack and then, a split-second later, the melodic scrape of metal on metal, followed by a final pained groan.*

His eyes opening, Thor looked up at Odin with a tearful gaze, his chest tightening as the memory played over and over in his mind.

"Sága," Thor said.

Thor woke to the flash of cameras above him.

He squinted, whipping his head around to take stock of his surroundings. Sif was by his side, lying with him in the broken concrete in front of a shop that made what he and many of his Midgard friends considered to be the best slice in Brooklyn. Sif was burned from the explosion, her skin red and crusted with blood, but from the pain that even the slightest movement sent through Thor's body, he knew he was charred just as badly. She was breathing, though, which made Thor smile. Of all the places to end up, it was here— the last place he'd visited. He could have chosen to interpret it as some quirk of the bridge's magic, regurgitating its last accessed location in its final moments, but instead, Thor chose to think of it as a sign.

He and Sif were *supposed* to be here.

That thought was all that could get him through the pain both physical and otherwise, as he was flooded with memories of Sága. He remembered what seemed to be another life layered on top of his own—a life with a dear friend who, until hours ago, did not exist in his mind. With those memories—games by the lake, a secret shared in confidence, and then a final, guilt-ridden betrayal—it wasn't just Sága the person who Thor remembered. He remembered how it felt to love her.

In those memories, which felt *right* if not his own, he loved Sága every bit as much as Volstagg, as Hogun, as Fandral. His heart was heavy as he thought of what must have happened since these memories to turn his dear friend into the hateful assassin he left in Asgard.

The group of people surrounding Thor and Sif, snapping pictures with their phones, backed up as he stood, helping his sputtering friend to her feet. It was easy to be rude to an Asgardian when they were lying in a pile of rubble, but when they stood two heads above you, it seemed like less of a good idea.

Not everyone stepped back, though. A woman wearing a hooded jacket stayed close to Thor and Sif, scoping the scene with a skeptical eye, while reaching into her belt. She leaned into them and then, her eyes wide from behind a gleaming golden mask, began to withdraw a pistol.

"Madame Masque," Thor growled. "Take your hand off that weapon or feel the wrath of an angry god."

Without a moment's pause, Masque turned away and

broke into a run as Thor stood, his legs shaking, pain shooting through his body, holding out his hammer in her direction.

"Stop where you stand," Thor bellowed. "Or, by the sacred bridge that once connected the stars, you will fall."

CHAPTER TEN

ODINSON

Sága gazed down on the Kingdom of Asgard from above as its king, joined by a limping Loki, looked at his courtyard in devastation. Standing out of sight, perched on the hills in which, years ago, a secret she had confided in Thor had sealed her fate, Sága watched, a smile gracing her lips, as Odin stumbled toward the entryway to his castle, his path blocked with his guards' bodies. From the distance, in their golden armor, they looked like piles of coins cast onto the ground.

Sága had no quarrel with the guards. That's why they were allowed to perish. It was a shame that both Thor and Sif were now gone, but Sága could still move on. As much as she hated them for their betrayal, they weren't the worst of those who had wronged her. Sif was a pawn in a larger game, and Thor, Sága knew, of course, that his folly was his pride. He had spoken her name to Odin and that had started it all, yes, but he did so without malice.

And for what he did after that, Sága would never say that

he deserved anything better than a painful death, but she was not interested in his suffering.

It was the two below, Odin and Loki, who walked together, reunited as father and son in the wake of Sága's attack. Loki, whom Sága had loved above all, her friend and her confidant and her future. Loki, who had abandoned her in favor of schemes to move the hearts of a father he claimed to hate and a brother he swore was his lesser. While Sága suffered, Loki sought his own selfish interests and then, after her banishment, forgot her like the rest of them.

And Odin, oh, she would relish his ultimate fate. She could scarcely wait to see the light drain from his eyes as she carried out her endgame. The All-Father had seen wars in his lifetime that shook the very roots of the World Tree, Yggdrasil, but there would be no more war in Asgard. No more bloodshed. No more fighting.

Asgard, very soon, would go to sleep. It would never awaken.

"ODIN!"

The All-Father looked skyward as the familiar voice rang through the night. His eye settled upon a dark figure poised high on one of Asgard's largest hilltops. No sooner had he spotted her than she was on the move, speeding toward them. She leapt from the hills and into the valley that ramped down into Odin's courtyard, where his guards' bodies were scattered.

"Her strength is incredible," Loki snarled. "Before I could even act, she merely touched your little toy Destroyers and siphoned their power into her body. Can she do that with anything, old man?"

"That wasn't always the case," Odin said.

"I know that now!" Loki barked, his eyes darting about. He, like Odin, was looking for Sága, to anticipate whatever devastating attack she planned. Odin knew that if she had breached his castle, as it had appeared, there was nothing they could do to brace themselves for the onslaught to come.

Odin kept his voice low, scanning the area for their assailant. "Do you remember now, Son?"

"Bits and pieces," Loki said. "How is it that this has happened? I would've known. I would've—I would've *remembered*. Not even *you* are capable of such trickery to—"

"To trick the Trickster himself?" Odin asked. "Oh, but there are still secrets within Asgard, Loki, that escape your prying eyes. Secrets with great power. Though, now, one more lies broken."

"That stone." Loki's lips curled into a sneer.

"The Obsidian Tablet," Odin said. He pointed to the forest, where he saw a dark shape barreling toward them. "A last resort for the desperate, and, now I know, a foolish recourse at that."

"I was able to access the tablet without resistance," Loki snarled. "*Anyone* in the realm of Asgard could have done so. You keep this vicious creature locked away just out of sight, so that anyone ignorant to the truth of what she is could free her? Are you mad?"

"Not anyone," Odin said, looking up at Loki, whose green eyes burned. "Only an Odinson could gain access to that chamber. Anyone else would have been obliterated by my guard. You are, Loki, as much as you may hate me, my Son."

Loki's stony stare faltered for a moment before he stepped back from Odin, letting out a hiss of breath. "You say this to place blame upon me for her release. Had you shared the *truth* with me, or even that fool *Thor*, perhaps—"

"We both might be safe now," Odin said as Sága ran past the gate, coming right at them. "I believe that you, Loki, of all people, would have released her if you'd known the truth."

"You think me pure evil," Loki said.

"No, Loki," the All-Father replied. "I don't think you could have borne to let her suffer."

Sága came to a stop in front of Odin and Loki, staring at them through squinted eyes. Odin looked older than the man who had stuffed her into a sarcophagus and condemned her to a life of silent, lonely torture under the weight of the Obsidian Tablet. He looked white and old and tired, and *gods* did Sága love it. The All-Father had used time to torture her, and look what time had done to him.

Loki looked much like Sága remembered. When she'd first risen from her sarcophagus, she'd lashed out in a rage. She'd looked at him, of course, but she hadn't taken the time to drink him in. Now, as he stood, staring at her from the eyes she'd known since she was a little girl, she wondered how much he remembered.

Because she remembered it all.

"Thor . . ." Sága said, her voice thick as she stared at Loki, "is *dead*."

Loki sputtered out a laugh that didn't reach his eyes. He may have been able to trick his father and brother in the days when she called him a friend, but Loki's eyes always betrayed his truth to Sága. As she stared at him, the silence stretching between them, she watched the Trickster's face twist from a pained, faux grin to an expression of blank disbelief.

"You lie," Loki said with the air of someone trying to convince himself.

Next to him, Odin looked weak, as if he was about to fall to his knees. Sága laughed as Loki grabbed his dazed father on either side of his face, screaming at him.

"No!" Loki screamed. "If you fall into the Odinsleep now, old man, I will rip your beating heart from your chest."

Odin didn't resist Loki's grasp. He just murmured, "She speaks true. She speaks true."

Sága walked slowly toward Loki, who pushed himself off of Odin. Loki shook his head, pulling his lips back in a scornful sneer. "No. I don't believe it. Thor—Thor wouldn't fall to *you*. You couldn't even kick your way out of a box. You—"

Sága lunged forward and grabbed Loki by the throat, squeezing him into silence. Loki, his eyes shining and bloodshot, looked down at her from his bloody, beaten face as she lifted him off of the ground.

"Will you cry for him?" Sága asked. "It has been a long time since we've shared our secrets, Loki. What have I taken from you by murdering your brother?"

She felt Loki's throat vibrate in her grip as he tried to respond, his face twisted in agony and hatred, but only choked squeaks came out.

"Have you built bridges with him in the time I've been gone, or have you just burned them all as you were so keen to do as a boy?" Sága asked. "Did Thor die with love in his heart for you as his brother or did he turn to ash thinking of you as nothing but a problem? A disappointment?"

Sága felt a powerful blow to the small of her back. It sent her flying forward, Loki still in her grasp. As they hit the ground, Loki rolled over, using his momentum to break free. Sága leapt to her feet and saw Odin running at her from the side, lifting his blade high.

"LOKI!" Odin bellowed. "AVENGE YOUR BROTHER! FIGHT WITH ME, MY SON!"

He brought the blade down on Sága, who crossed her arms over her head, blocking the strike. Even with the power of the stolen magic flowing through her veins, she felt a warm splash of blood as the blade dug into her flesh. She ripped her bleeding arm from the sword and shot her elbow back, cracking Odin in his eye.

Odin swung the blade again, this time at her stomach. Sága leapt backward to avoid the slash, but this time found herself in Loki's arms.

Loki grabbed Sága's neck in one hand and palmed the back of her head with his other. He twisted sharply in an attempt to break her neck, but all Sága felt was a satisfying pop. She grinned and slammed her face into Loki's, sending him stumbling back. He steadied his footing and, as Sága ran toward him, waved his hands. Sága's vision was suddenly filled with green, as duplicate visions of Loki appeared, surrounding her. The replicas danced around her, sneering and laughing as she waved her hands through them, searching for the real one.

Instead, a gleaming golden gauntlet burst through one of the mirage's chests and caught her in the throat. Pain rushed through Sága's neck as she felt her throat close up from the force of the punch, but she didn't pause. She rolled out of the way as Odin's sword cut through another of the fake Lokis, cutting into the stone where she had just been standing.

One of the Lokis rushed at her, and Sága flinched when it passed through her, laughing. She ducked a broad sword stroke from Odin, and saw, out of the corner of her eye, two of the Lokis charging at her. Not to be tricked again, Sága turned her focus to Odin, preparing to block him as he charged her head on with his sword.

As she shot out her arms and turned to the side to smack away Odin's blade, she felt a sharp blow from the side.

The real Loki grinned at her wildly, his eyes streaming with tears as the two of them fell together. He held on tightly to one of the fallen guards' swords, which he'd buried to the hilt in Sága's rib cage. Sága stared up at him, his face close to hers, his sweaty black hair hanging down in stands. His chin trembled.

Blood pooled out from Sága's wound. She tried to speak, but found that her voice was no more than a hoarse creak. Unbelievable, ripping pain shot through her body, followed quickly by numbness.

"FOR THOR!"

Odin pointed his own blade at Sága's throat. Loki stepped back, leaving the guard's sword in her side.

"Do it," Loki hissed.

Odin glared at Sága, his armed locked out as the sword grazed her neck. "She's already dead, Son."

"She murdered him!" Loki barked, his voice breaking. "Your precious son lies dead by her hand and you wish to give her the dignity of a quiet death? Take your vengeance."

Sága looked up at Odin, her entire body tingling with numbness. She wondered if he'd do it. It would make a certain kind of morbid sense, after all of this, that Odin and Loki were the ones to survive. They'd been the ones who had been the worst to her, of course, and if she couldn't complete her crusade as she'd planned, at least Odin and Loki would be alive to suffer through the devastation she'd caused.

The hilt of the sword fell to the stone pathway with a clatter.

Sága looked at it, confused for a moment as she saw the remains of the blade disintegrating in her blood. With a deep gasp, air filled her lungs and the numbness that had spread through her body burst out of her in a cloud of glittering magic—a mixture of Bifrost power and other stolen magic. She felt the lips of her wound touch and the skin reform. The searing pain, in an instant, was gone.

Odin, his eyes wide, charged forward with the blade, but Sága was already gone. She threw herself to the side and eyed a fallen guard. She grabbed his sword and shield and sprinted toward Odin and Loki, who stared at her as if she were Surtur himself.

Sága spun around and flung the shield at Loki. It cracked into his head and, instantly unconscious, the Trickster crumbled next to his astonished father. Odin, roaring, charged toward Sága with his own blade.

Sága met the strike of his sword with one of her own. Their blades clashed, the sounds ringing out into the night as they dueled on the path littered with Odin's dead guards.

"The magic you've stolen," Odin said, lashing out his sword, "it will eat you alive. No Asgardian should be able to do what you've done. If your blood burns Uru, what will it do to your flesh and bones?"

"I am *more* than flesh and bone now," Sága said, parrying his strikes. "I'm a conduit, thanks to you."

"I did *not* make you into this," Odin said. "I only did what I felt to be best for my kingdom. I—"

"LOOK AT YOUR KINGDOM NOW!" Sága swung her sword down, hard. The blade caught Odin's hand, sending his sword flying with a trail of blood. Odin grasped his bleeding palm as Sága advanced on him, swinging her sword at his legs.

Odin fell as the arc of her blade cut into his thighs. As he hit the ground, Sága pounced on him, throwing her weapon to the side. She dug her forearm into his neck, ropes of dirty blonde hair hanging as she stared at the All-Father's white face.

She held her arm in place until Odin's eye rolled back into his head and his lid fluttered closed, revealing only a slit of white.

"Say good night, my king," Sága said, "to the Asgard you knew."

CHAPTER ELEVEN

A CONVERSATION OVER PIZZA

Thor sat next to Sif in a pizza parlor. Madame Masque stared across at them from behind her golden mask, eyes wild. Thor took a bite from his slice, dismayed to find that even his tongue had been burned from the explosion. Around them, the pizzeria was full of people continuing to snap pictures of this strange trio. Normally, Thor would have asked them to stop, if only for the sake of the employees' sanity, but with the very fate of Asgard hanging in the balance and no way of getting back to save the Realm Eternal, Thor hadn't yet found the energy to shoo the onlookers away.

"What in the world happened to you?" Masque snapped.

"Speak when spoken to," Thor said, swallowing. He dropped the slice back on his plate and looked at Masque. It felt absolutely bizarre to go from facing down the unstoppable Sága, as she laid her wrath down upon Asgard, to sitting here across from Masque, tomato sauce on his lips. He knew that Sif, and perhaps all of the people around them, thought he was crazy. The truth was, if Thor gave up on his home realm now, he would fall to despair, so while he was banished here on Earth, unable to get back to Asgard until the Rainbow Bridge was somehow rebuilt, he would continue to act as if he would make his way home. And when he returned home, he knew it wasn't just Sága he'd have to contend with. Loki had been up to something here on Earth, and it coincided far too well with Sága's release to be coincidental.

"I knew you'd come looking for me," Masque hissed.

"It was you, Masque, who seemed ready to shoot me on the ground," Thor said.

"Because you Avengers can't take a win. You have to dominate us. Chase us around like rats until we have to show ourselves," Masque said. "You already sent Parker to S.H.I.E.L.D. You took us down, yet again. And then you show up right behind me when I'm getting ready to leave this wretched city behind once and for all. Don't pretend that it's coincidence."

Thor didn't bother to correct her. Of course, she happened to be in the wrong place at the wrong time—though, perhaps, during better days, Thor would have believed that the universe had put him here, with Masque, so he could learn something. He didn't know if he believed that anymore, all he had was a glimmer of hope and the time to find out if it was more than just a flash in the dark.

"Believe what you want. I have no interest in harming you, Masque. Only in your truth," Thor said.

"What?"

"Loki may be my brother, but he is no friend of Asgard," Thor said. "Tell me, Masque, what did he say to you that led to the other day's conflict?"

"Will you let me go if I do?" Masque asked.

"No."

"Then why should I?"

"Because," Thor said, "as you can see, I am in the middle of what you might call a crisis. I'm furious, Masque. I do not wish to unleash those feelings. But if you get in my way, I will have no other recourse. Tell me what Loki said. He is no friend of yours."

Masque looked toward the group of onlookers. "If they leave."

Thor nodded. He slid out of his seat, stood, and addressed the group of people gathered around them. Thor held Mjolnir out to them, smiling as widely as he could. His cheeks ripped with pain.

"Touch the mighty Mjolnir, and then go," Thor said. "On the way out, if you would, please tip the kind people that work here. They have put up with much on this day, and they make a fine slice."

As the group flooded toward the counter, Thor returned to his seat. Masque leered at him. "They listen to you," she said.

"Aye."

"Why?" she asked. "I've always wondered: what is it about

you and Captain America that people look up to? People can't relate to you. You're a god! You fly through the air and you—you *smite* and you think you're above it all. *Why* you?"

Thor looked to Sif, who wanted to reach across the table and strangle Madame Masque.

"I don't ask for reverence," Thor said. "Nor power, nor respect. I am a guest on Earth, and it has become a second, most dear, home. But I have another home, and it is in danger now. So I ask you one more time, Masque. Tell me what Loki said."

She nodded. "Fine. He said that together, we could all take down the Avengers."

"Is that all he said?" Sif asked. "Loki wanted to join with your team?"

"Yes," Masque said. "And we declined. Loki brings misery wherever he goes."

Thor narrowed his eyes. "Understand that if I find out you conspired with my brother to harm Earth or Asgard, I will treat you as an enemy of the Realm Eternal. This you do not want."

She looked away from him and Thor knew that she was telling the truth. She knew nothing that could help them in any way.

Masque remained silent as Thor borrowed the pizzeria's phone to call Maria Hill over at S.H.I.E.L.D. Madame Masque didn't say another word as they waited for

S.H.I.E.L.D. to cart her off to the same facility where the Hood was being detained. After speaking to Maria Hill and dodging questions about their injuries, Thor and Sif left, turning down an alley for a moment of privacy.

"That was a waste of time," Sif said. "We learned nothing."

"No," Thor said. "We learned that the events on Earth have no involvement in Sága's release on Asgard. Loki made his enemies here in pursuit of the same goal he always chases."

"Chaos?" Sif asked.

Thor sighed. "My destruction. I believe that he may have known of Sága. If anyone could've divined the truth, it would be Loki. Perhaps, releasing her was a last resort to—"

"To what, Thor?" Sif asked. "Loki doesn't want you dead."

"I'm sure that you are wrong," Thor said. "But let us save that conversation for later. We must find our way back to Asgard as quickly as possible. I fear for our home in our absence, Sif. I feel Asgard bleed."

"As do I," Sif said. "Where shall we go?"

"To assemble the Avengers," Thor said, inclining his chin toward the sky.

"What did you do?!"

Loki charged across the yard toward Thor, his eyes blood-shot as tears streamed down his face. Thor, who had been reclining on the warm grass, soaking in the midday sun with Sif, propped himself up on his elbow. He watched his fuming brother march toward them, kicking up clods of dirt with each step.

"What riles you so, Loki?" Thor said, with a rolling chuckle. "You've been released from your cell today—and if I were our father, I would've kept you down there for longer."

"It's not funny, Thor," Sif said. "Men are dead."

Sighing, Thor climbed to his feet, just in time for Loki to grab him by the neck. Thor shot his hands out, sending his younger brother flying. Loki landed in a heap a few yards away, but bounced right back up, marching toward Thor.

"Don't make me show you how seriously I take your deceit, Brother," Thor said, pointing to Loki. *The young Trickster stopped in his tracks, but stared at Thor with murder in his eyes.*

"It wasn't my fault," Loki snapped. "It was you."

"Me?!" Thor said, unable to hold back a chiding laugh. "You build bridges of lies to avoid the truth, Loki. Those guards are dead because of your foolishness."

Loki spat, a disgusted sneer spreading over his face. "I speak not of the guards, Brother. What of Sága?"

"What of Sága?" Thor barked. "What does her punishment have to do with me?"

Sif stood, jumping between them. "Hold your tongue, Thor," *she said. She held out a hand toward Loki—something halfway* between a calming gesture and a warning. "Speak from your heart, Loki. It is animosity and anger that led us here to begin with. Thor is your brother, and you are of Asgard. Speak, friend. Let us understand your rage."

"You can't hide the revulsion from your eyes, Sif," Loki said. "You call me 'friend' but I've only ever known one. And now, she is gone, left to rot in the darkness of Niffleheim."

"Niffleheim?" Thor said, incredulous. "Impossible. She was sent to serve her punishment in Odin's royal cells with you. I'm surprised you were released first, considering the gravity of your ill deeds."

"Thor," Sif snapped.

"She was not with me," Loki retorted. "I sat alone in my cell for weeks, next to criminals of the worst kind. Mother visited me, and Father released me only to tell me the truth of what he has done to her."

"He wouldn't," Thor said. "Niffleheim? For withholding the truth of your trickery? A punishment only a mad tyrant would . . ."

Thor trailed off, staring at his brother's heaving chest and shining, wet cheeks. Sif, her black hair framing her pale, nervous face, turned to Thor.

"Would he?" Sif whispered.

Niffleheim was one of the Nine Worlds, an icy and dark realm of death and danger. Niffleheim was home to a region called Hel, ruled by the wicked Hela, which served as a pit of *trials and suffering for the wicked after death. It wasn't just Hel that made the realm of Niffleheim a punishment too harsh for a girl of Sága's years, though. The realm was a place of death and decay that claimed as many minds as it did lives.*

"He would and he did," Loki snarled. "He told me himself. He took me out of my cell and said that it was I who put Sága there, and that when she came back, both she and I will have learned a lesson."

Thor stared at his brother, a heavy sinking feeling in his stomach.

"And I have learned a lesson," Loki continued. "Odin is exactly the mad tyrant you fear now, Brother. Is his truly the seat you wish to fill? Because I promise you . . . if it is . . . you will find yourself with an enemy in me unlike any you or any previous king has ever faced."

Thor took a step forward, his voice softening. "Loki—"

Loki jerked backward. "She'll be back. If anything happens to her there, while chained to whatever rock that devil on the throne locked her to, this is my vow: the next time I attack Asgard, it will not be a child's trick." He turned to walk away but, after a few paces, stopped. "I cannot hate you for saying her name. You foolishly hoped that the old man would be better than he is, but maybe, maybe now you see what I see. She didn't deserve it, Thor."

Thor, with Sif by his side, watched Loki walk away from the castle until he disappeared in the darkness of the woods.

• • •

Thor felt Sif's eyes on him as they walked into the ground entrance to Stark Tower.

"Are my wounds as grievous as they feel?" Thor asked. His voice echoed softly through the large expanse of Tony's lobby, where a floating robot approached them, blinking with red.

"No more than mine," Sif said, her tone gentle. "What were you thinking about, Thor?"

Thor gestured for Sif to look ahead as F.R.I.D.A.Y.'s facial recognition software swept over his face from the floating bot. The interior glow turned green.

"Welcome back, Thor," F.R.I.D.A.Y. said. The lights shifted to red once again and moved over Sif's face.

"Welcome from Asgard, Lady Sif," F.R.I.D.A.Y. said. "We will have you both taken care of in the infirmary right away. Mr. Stark will meet you there."

"Have you been having them as well?" Thor asked. "These—waking dreams? No, that's not right. I don't have the word for them."

"I have," Sif said. "They're memories, Thor."

Thor shook his head, feeling the burned skin stretch as he did so. He hoped the infirmary was loaded with enough painkillers for two Asgardians. "Memories, yes, but I feel helpless. As if I'm watching myself go through pain I've never had to deal with. I can't act, can't change things. I've never felt anything like this."

"Do you remember all of it now?" Sif asked.

"I don't know," Thor said. "I do not believe so. I know that my father banished Sága to Niffleheim for a time, but that was when we were still young. And we *remembered* her, there was no—no spell, no deceit. Father *told* Loki what he'd done then. How Sága acquired her powers, why we came to forget her, how she was locked in the sarcophagus, holed away leagues under Asgard—it all remains a mystery."

"As painful as it is, Thor, I think it best we try to focus on remembering," Sif said. "If we unlock the truth, we can divine some way of . . ."

She trailed off, a troubled look passing through her gaze.

"Some way of *what*?" Thor pressed. "We don't know what happened that made her do this. She believes that we deserve this, this crusade of hers."

"There's one thing about my memories of Sága that truly frightens me," Sif said.

"What is that?"

"She seems smart," Sif said. "Smart, kind, and empathetic. No more insane or cruel than you or me."

Before Thor could reply, the elevator doors opened into the white, sterile walls of the Stark Tower hospital wing. Tony Stark, with two sleek, unmanned Iron Man models behind him, walked over to Thor, wincing.

"Yeesh," Tony said, touching Thor's cheek. Thor withdrew from the pain, letting out a burst of air through his teeth.

"Stark!" Thor hissed.

"Ah," Tony said, cringing as he held up his hands in innocence. "Sorry. Couldn't help myself. I'm sure it's very painful." He turned to Sif, looking her up and down with another cringe. "Sif, always nice to see you. You're looking, well, medium rare."

Sif stared at Tony, deadpan.

"Right, right, barbecued gods not in the mood for the banter, got it," he said. "Come with me."

Thor and Sif followed Tony into the infirmary. The two Asgardians sat on the cushioned hospital beds as the unmanned Iron Man suits prepared two injections.

"Needles?" Sif asked.

"Not a fan?" Tony said. "When I was a kid, I used to be terrified of shots. My mom would sing me a song when the needle was coming, and it would distract me. A little. Sometimes, the vein was hard to find and they'd just stick me and stick me over and over like a little precocious pincushion."

"Stark," Thor said.

"Yeah?"

"You are not improving the situation."

"Pincushion talk aside," Tony said, "I could, you know, sing to you. A little Sabbath, maybe, just until the needle pricks the skin."

"I shall take the needle over the song," Sif said, holding out her arm. "I mean no offense."

Tony shrugged. "Your loss."

Thor watched Sif wince as the needle pieced her skin, injecting an amber liquid into her vein. He held out his arm and felt a slight pop as the sharp syringe pierced his thick skin and filled his bloodstream with the same fluid.

"This will expedite the healing process," F.R.I.D.A.Y. said. "After a short sleep, you should feel rejuvenated. While you won't be entirely healed, this serum will send a signal to your sensory receptors that will block your pain without numbing you. Once you wake up, you'll be good to go."

"Albeit not as pretty as usual," Tony said, casting a smarmy look toward Thor.

"There is something about these tiny blades," Sif said, with a shudder as the needles withdrew from both her and Thor's arms. "I'd face a storm of one hundred swords before one of these."

"Kinda looks like you *did*," Tony said. "Flaming swords, maybe. What happened to you two? This is Loki's work, yeah?"

"No," Thor said. Then, pausing, he reconsidered. "Perhaps, in a way. I'm uncertain. We have much to share with you, Stark. Is Banner still here?"

"Yes," Tony said. "He's in the lab with Stephen."

"Stephen!" Thor marked, his eyes going wide. "Doctor Strange is in the building?"

"What are you, a DJ? Yes, Doctor Strange is *in the building!*" Tony said. He smiled and patted Thor on the shoulder, but Thor used his waning strength to grab his friend's wrist.

"Tell Strange . . ." Thor said, his eyelids growing heavy as the injection began to take over, pulling him into the world of dreams. "That we have to rebuild the Rainbow Bridge."

The last thing Thor saw before his vision faded was Tony looking at him with a furrowed brow, his lips moving but no sound coming out. Thor descended into darkness.

Thunder boomed in the distance as she stalked toward him. Thor felt blood pouring from a wound in his side, but he knew that pausing to investigate could cost him his life. There had been enough death on this day.

Sága leapt over the crumpled form of Frigga and landed in front of Thor, who stood guarding the entrance to Odin's room of treasures. The Destroyer had been sapped of its immense power, which was now within Sága. She had used it to unleash a sneak attack on Asgard, killing and maiming wherever she could go.

Thor swung Mjolnir at Sága, who dipped to avoid the blow. She caught Thor in the stomach with a flurry of punches that drove him back against the door to the vault. Sága jumped past him and latched onto the thick door, trying to pry it open with her hands.

"NO!" Thor bellowed, holding out his hammer. An incredible bolt of lightning, bigger than any he'd ever gathered in his young years, collected on Mjolnir and rocketed toward Sága. As it hit her, she convulsed in midair, still hanging on to the door of the vault.

Thor jumped up toward her, grabbing his friend by the torso. Together, the two of them fell to the ground. Thor placed his hammer on Sága's chest, knowing that she would be unable to lift it.

Thor collapsed next to Sága, who kicked and screamed, writhing in attempt to get Mjolnir off of her. It was in vain, though. As long as he left the hammer there, she would be pinned to the ground. It seemed to be the one mystical item in all of Asgard that her new, wicked powers didn't allow her to drain.

"Why, Sága?" Thor asked, his breath ragged. "What demon has overtaken you? If you can hear me, please speak to me. Fight through."

Sága fell silent, turning to Thor. Flecks of blood dotted her cheeks under eyes dark with bags. They'd fought all night, after a day of sneak attacks by Sága. Thor couldn't fathom how many of his people were dead. His mother, Frigga, was alive, but left with ragged breath, her chest barely rising and falling. He could scarcely imagine what he'd do to the person he once called his friend if she'd have ripped out her throat the same way she'd done to Odin's guards.

"Look at me," she rasped.

Thor snorted. "All day, I've done nothing but look at you attacking me and the realm I love."

"Then you ignore what is plain before your eyes! There is no demon within me," Sága said. "I took a gamble on my exile and I fought for these powers, but do you not see the truth in my eyes? In my face?"

Thor was afraid of the answer.

"How long have I been gone, Thor?" she asked.

"Three weeks," Thor said. "Three weeks and two days."

Sága closed her eyes, gritting her teeth. "No wonder. Look at you, Thor. Still a boy."

"What do you mean?" Thor asked.

"AWAY!" The voice boomed down the hall. Thor, bracing himself for another attack, spun around to see not an assailant, but his father bounding down the corridor. He was backed up by a lineup of Asgardian warriors, many of them bleeding and beaten. Odin himself had a gash in his head—Thor had witnessed Sága deal that blow to him. After her sneak attacks, she had stormed the kingdom wearing the armor of one of the guards she'd killed. As Odin assembled his men, unaware that his target was among them, Sága snatched his scepter and cracked him over the head with it until she was pulled off by his guards. Soon after, they laid broken and she returned to finish Odin's punishment. Thor had heard the commotion and came to stop her—that's when their fight had begun. When it became clear that Thor was going to win, Sága pushed toward Odin's treasure trove, and though Thor was confused as to how she was absorbing all of that magical power, he knew that letting her gain access to that room would mean his certain death. And Odin's as well.

Alas, here Odin stood over the defeated Sága and the exhausted Thor. He pointed down at Sága, a purple gem floating out of his palm. Sága's eyes glowed purple for a moment and then shut. Her head fell limp, lolling to the side.

"Father!" Thor cried. "Is she—"

"She lives," Odin said, lifting the unconscious form of Frigga, who stirred in her husband's arms. "Against my better judgment, she lives. Remove Mjolnir, my Son."

Thor leaned over to his fallen friend and plucked the hammer off of her chest. Indeed, she was breathing, but it was cold comfort in the wake of what had just happened. He watched in silence as two of Odin's men hoisted Sága up and carried her away, to who knew where.

Odin turned to go, but Thor called after him.

"She looked—"

The All-Father turned to Thor, peering at him over his shoulder. "Yes, boy?"

"She was there for a long time, wasn't she?" Thor asked. "She looked different. Older."

For a stretch of time, Odin stared at his son, his eye gleaming. Next to him, in his arms, Frigga cleared her throat, her voice strained.

"You should rest," she said. "We all should."

"Tell me!" Thor insisted. "It was I who spoke her name to you. This is on ME! I must know the truth."

"There is something that you must know about your brother," Odin said at last, his tone measured. "There are two directions Loki can take. One of those directions leads to darkness for all of us. I have seen that darkness within him, and I am doing everything I can to steer him down the right path. Sága played a part in pushing him toward darkness. She knew not what she did, because she was just a girl. Loki, just a boy. I needed Sága to learn, to understand what she had done, to understand the truth about Loki while she was away."

"How long?" Thor asked.

"Thor . . ."

"HOW LONG!? You worked some kind of spell to make her life drag on in seclusion while we in Asgard lived a mere three weeks!" Thor barked. "How long did she suffer in Niffleheim for the sin of trusting me with Loki's plan?"

Odin opened his mouth to yell at Thor, an expression that the young Asgardian knew well. However, Odin seemed to rethink it, and shrunk before Thor, his shoulders falling and his chest deflating. For the first time, he looked like an old man.

"It was a mistake," Odin said. "I—"

The sentence remained unfinished, as Odin turned around, leading Frigga away from Thor. Unable to support himself on his legs, Thor fell. It felt as if the world was spinning around him. He knew not how Sága did what she did, but she had thought that he, Loki, and their friends had let her agonize in solitude for what had to be years and years. If it was true, that she hadn't been taken over by a demon but instead sought her new, terrifying powers, Thor wasn't sure he could blame her.

The men she killed didn't deserve to die. They played no part in this. That was on Odin and he, himself.

"I told you."

Thor didn't have to look up to know who it was. Loki's oily voice was distinct enough, but for all Thor felt, it could've been his own thoughts speaking aloud to him. Loki was right.

Thor didn't say that, though. Instead, he sat, staring at the bloody floor as Loki strode over to him. When Thor looked up, he saw that Loki, too, had been brutalized. His face was a mess of bumps and cuts, one of his eyes swollen entirely shut. He was bent over, hunched from the pain, and his arm was bent at a strange angle. He'd gotten it the worst of all of them—of all the survivors, at least.

"Loki, my brother," Thor said, alarmed. "Let me get you help."

"Don't," Loki said, his chin trembling. "I don't want to go to him. Look what he did, Thor. Look what he turned her into."

Thor had nothing to say. He felt like he should hug Loki, but

PAT SHAND

he knew that if it didn't break Loki's battered body, Loki might well stab him for the act.

*"He says he's sparing her, Thor, but he's going to kill her,"
Loki said. "Tomorrow, I swear to you, Asgard will be draped
in black and we will mourn not only the loss of life at Sága's
hands, but her life at those of the All-Father. We cannot let him
do this to her. This is where we take a stand."*

*Thor studied Loki, wishing he knew what to say to his
brother. He wanted to offer comforting words, to promise that
they'd either be able to stop their father or that, somehow,
everything would be okay. Thor said the first thing that came
to his mind. The words tumbled out of his mouth, sloppy and
strained.*

"And do what?" Thor asked.

*Loki glowered at him, and Thor knew that he'd misspoken.
He sputtered to say something else, but in a turn of his emerald
cape, Loki disappeared into thin air.*

*Thor held his knees alone in the corridor, weeping. He
didn't know exactly what he'd lost quite yet, but he knew in
the pit of his gut that, from this day forward, life would never
be the same.*

Thor slowly opened his eyes. The first thing he saw was
his hand, still red and a little raw, but no longer horribly
blistered. Sif held Thor's beefy fingers between her own,

rubbing them. It was then that Thor noticed that his cheeks were wet.

He snatched his hand away from Sif's and pawed at his face, scooting up in bed. It didn't hurt so much to move anymore, so Stark's serum had worked, but there was nothing so painful to the God of Thunder as a bruised ego. He looked up at Sif with a bashful smile.

"It was a dream," he said. "Tears don't count if they're inspired by a dream."

Sif didn't smile. She took Thor's hand again, his throat tightening.

"I saw it, too," Sif said. "The attack. What happened to Sága. I think this memory might be the last one. I feel *different*."

"Aye," Thor said. "I do as well. He made her disappear. After her attack, he kept her alive but erased her from all of our memories. From the history of Asgard. And along with it, all of his own ill-conceived deeds that led to this. You know what this means, Sif."

Sif nodded, closing her eyes.

"All of this, all of this blood," Thor said. "It's on my father's hands. Once Sága is stopped, it is Odin who must face judgment for what has become of Asgard."

CHAPTER TWELVE
FINAL JUDGMENT

"How does it feel, old man?"

Loki grinned at Odin as the All-Father stirred. They were both, along with Frigga and the Warriors Three, pinned to the rocky wall of the cavern where Loki had first discovered Sága's sarcophagus. All of them but Loki, and now the slowly waking Odin, were unconscious. Their limbs were held in place by the remains of the Destroyer guards' armor, the pieces of which were bent around their wrists and ankles like cuffs that dug into the stone. All of them hung there, looking down at the platform below where Sága had been imprisoned in her casket for what Loki now knew had been ages. His memories had returned, and his hatred for his father had never been so potent.

Now, below them, the casket was gone. All that remained were the shattered chunks of what had been the Obsidian Tablet.

"Loki . . ." Odin rasped, pulling against the mystically enhanced shards of armor that pinned him against the wall.

"You can get us out of this. I know you have the power to do so."

"Do you know that?" Loki asked. "Tell me, Father, what else can I do to save us from the result of your mistakes?"

"You must listen to me, Son," Odin said. "Look around. Even if you care nothing for me, I know you still have love in your heart for your mother. Volstagg, Fandral, Hogun, you know that they do not deserve to die. If it is true, and your brother has truly fallen, honor him. *Stop* this."

Loki smiled from ear to ear. "If you don't think I've already tried to disappear, you're more foolish than I could've imagined. Had I the power to leave, I would be gone, and so would Mother. But you? You deserve whatever Sága has in mind for you. *Worse.* You should consider yourself lucky I can't free myself, or I would stand by her and watch you burn."

"I know you must hate me, my Son, but if we are to die here, together, understand that I did what I did for—"

"Don't you *dare* say that you did this for me!" Loki snarled. "You did this because you're a cruel, old man, short-sighted and weak. You didn't know how to make me live the rigid life of acquiescence and peace that you so desperately wanted—the ultimate victory over the Frost Giants, to raise their king Laufey's son as your own. To make him docile, subjugated."

"That wasn't what I wanted, Loki."

"Even in the face of certain death, you lie," Loki said, and then cackled. "I think that maybe even you believe what you're saying. How very sad. You might not be able to admit who you are, Odin, but I see you plain as day. You banished Sága to show me that anything I cherished, any small bit of happiness I could claim, would be *gone* the moment I stepped out of line."

"No, Loki."

"*Yes*," Loki hissed. "Oh yes, I know the truth, you malevolent old fool. I remember it all now. You let them take her away, knowing that you'd erase her from our memories, allowing her to live here, *alive* in her tomb. Why not kill her? Why not just give her the peace of death?"

"Because he wasn't thinking about me."

The voice came from above. Loki and Odin looked up to see Sága descending toward them from the winding, rocky path above. She walked slowly, the urgency from her earlier assault on Asgard gone, replaced now with a confident stride.

"Sága," Odin said. "Know that if I could take your banishment back, I would. I was misguided to send you to Niffleheim, and to allow time to pass differently for you. I shoulder no greater mistake as king."

Loki watched as Sága walked down the circling path. In a few more turns, she would be level with them on the platform.

"I wouldn't take it back," Sága said. "No, it was there that I learned the truth about you. I needed that. Otherwise, I would've knelt and bowed for the rest of my days to a man who looks at me, a fellow Asgardian, as less than nothing."

"It's not true," Odin said.

Loki looked toward Odin, desperate to reach out and strike the man. He felt violated, as if something absolutely essential to who he was had been taken away from him. His hands ached to squeeze Odin's throat.

"Don't speak to her," Loki growled. "You think that she will accept your lies after what you did? You gave her a fate worse than death. Worse than Hel. You—"

"His sins are *nothing*," Sága said, stepping onto the platform, "compared to *yours*, Loki."

She walked up to Loki, who looked at her with hurt confusion from the rocky wall. He couldn't move to reach out to her, but he desperately wanted to. He couldn't imagine how he could forget her, and he ached now for the memories that he'd lost. They were in his mind and heart again, but he had been robbed of them for all of those years of his life.

"Sága, I had no part in this," Loki said softly as Sága came close to him, almost nose to nose. "No part in any of it. My mind was violated. Treasured memories stolen. You were ripped away from me, and—"

"And you have died and come back," Sága said. "You have mastered all studies of magic and have eclipsed even the wisest of mystical sages. I know this because I have drained all of the magic from all of the artifacts I can find, and the magic of Asgard knows you well, Loki, as an *abuser*. Tell me this, old friend. If you can master magic, why were you unable to find me?"

"I-I didn't know where to look, of course," Loki sputtered. "I didn't know *to* look. You'd been erased—"

"Amazing," Sága said, spinning away from Loki. She grabbed a large slab of the Obsidian Tablet off of the ground, lifting the hefty rock up with ease. "You surpass all of the mystics in Asgard and yet can't dig up memories that you supposedly treasure. Here's a memory for you, Loki. Say out loud *why* I was banished to Niffleheim."

"Thor," Loki said. "Because Thor told Odin that you—"

"Thor is to blame, but not nearly as much as you," Sága said. "I am here because of you. I was tortured and burned and left to rot for years in Niffleheim because of you, and then I was dragged down here and made into *nothing* because of you. Blotted out from the history of Asgard. Do you know how that feels, Loki?"

Loki wanted to say *yes*, because he believed that he did. He stopped himself, though, for fear that Sága would lose her temper and put that slab through his skull.

"It feels," Sága said, walking toward Loki and Odin with the slab, "like being a ghost. After a while, even I started to wonder if I was ever real. If there was a life beyond perfect blackness. Can either of you even fathom the loneliness? Powerlessness?"

"No," Loki said. "I can't."

"Sága," Odin said. "What are you doing with the tablet?"

"The tablet's broken," Sága said. "Loki said my name and that was that. This right here, this rock? This is for *you*."

She pressed it against Odin's chest.

"Please," Odin said. "You can stop now, Sága. Allow me to right a past wrong. Let me help you."

"I *am* going to help you," Sága said, holding the shard of the tablet against Odin's chest. "I'm going to make you understand how it felt. I'm going to carve your names into the Obsidian Stone—one piece for each surviving soul in Asgard—and then, I'm going to leave you to rot. I will leave Asgard behind, and this realm will become nothing more than a graveyard, filled with stories that never get told, legends that are quickly forgotten, and names that no one remembers. You will be like I was . . . living ghosts."

She pushed the stone into Odin's chest, hard. Loki gritted his teeth, feeling the panic building. He, for the first time ever, had thought that maybe appealing to Sága with honesty would work. It seemed that his hopes were misplaced.

"You know what is coming, Odin. The Obsidian Tablet is *yours*. This piece of it, at least," Sága said. She held out her hand and the chunk of black, glistening stone stayed glued to Odin's chest. Sága's eyes flashed back. "Resist your fate and I'll put it through your wife's skull. Frigga is partially to blame as well for not keeping her mad king in check, but I'll gladly let her meet the graceful hand of death in order to make you understand. Do you accept your fate?"

Loki gritted his teeth, watching as Odin looked down at the chunk of the Obsidian Tablet mystically bound to his armored chest.

"*Do you?*" Sága barked.

"ANSWER HER!" Loki screamed, knowing that Sága's threats were more than just words.

Odin swallowed. "I do."

Sága breathed out a huge sigh, almost as if she was relieved. Smiling, she leaned toward Odin and, with a single finger, touched the shard of the Obsidian Tablet. Loki watched, fascinated, as she dug her fingernail into its surface, tracing out what looked to be a circle.

"You had a tool for this," Sága said to Odin. "Delicate and mystical. I don't need anything but my own hands. The power of the Bifrost is within me now. Maybe *that's* what you should've had your people guard. At least then they would've died for a reason."

Odin spoke quickly, as if he were rushing to get out each word. "Sága, please, understand that—"

Loki watched, amazed as his father's face froze in place as Sága removed her hand from the Obsidian Tablet. She snapped her fingers and the Uru bindings keeping Odin in place burst into glittering dust. The All-Father slid down the cavern wall with a sudden weightlessness, like a leaf. He slowly fell on his back, with the tablet on his chest facing up. His skin was drained of color, and his single eye was now milky white.

Confused, Loki looked at him. The chunk of the Obsidian Tablet on his chest had a single word emblazoned upon it, glowing golden, pulsing bright then dim like a heartbeat. It read *Odin*.

"What is the problem, Loki?" Sága asked, her grin widening.

Loki stared down at the old man. He looked from the stone, to Sága, to his mother, and back to Sága, his mind racing.

"Who *is* that?" Loki asked.

Sága closed her eyes, smiling contentedly. "Thank you, Loki. Now, it's your turn."

To avoid the pain coursing through his skull, Thor stared at the Eye of Agamotto. The powerful amulet hung from Doctor Strange's neck, reflecting the fiery glow that blazed from his hands as he gripped Thor and Sif's heads. What began as a tingling sensation now felt like hot knives digging into Thor's brain from all directions. From Sif's screwed-up expression as she knelt next to him, he knew she felt the same.

Doctor Strange wore a flowing blue robe and a crimson cape, its high collar reaching up to border the sides of his pensive face. He had black hair with silver streaks on his temples, and gray eyes that Thor knew saw beyond what even the most wise Asgardians could fathom. Stephen Strange was the Sorcerer Supreme, the greatest practitioner of the mystic arts in all of existence.

If anyone could help, it was him.

"I am sorry, my friends," Doctor Strange said, a light, airy whisper. "Just a little more—"

Thor gave up on distracting himself and let the pain wash over him. At least he was alive to feel it; he did not know if he could say the same for anyone else in Asgard. The digging, grinding agony of Strange's spell built until Thor wondered if his fellow Avenger had actually inserted his fingers into his skull, and then, in an instant, burst into a cool release, as if he had been doused with mist.

Doctor Strange pulled back from Thor and Sif, slowly lowering his hands. Thor felt dizzy for a second, thinking he was about to pass out on the floor of Stark's training room, but found that, just a moment later, he was all right. Sif rose to her feet and held out a hand to Thor, who gladly took it, allowing her to pull him to his feet. Thor looked at Strange expectantly, as the Sorcerer Supreme lifted both hands, his index and middle fingers pointed outward toward his temple.

"Do you think you can do it?" Thor asked.

"Yes," Strange said, closing his eyes. His fingertips glowed all of the colors of the Bifrost, and Thor's heart stirred with hope. "The problem at the moment is, though, that I'm uncertain if I'll be able to get it done *today*, or over the course of seven years."

Thor threw back his head is despair. So much for hope. "My friend, this is not good news. Sága ravages Asgard as we speak, and I fear her crusade may be a righteous one. We have to stop her before she does something to the Realm Eternal that cannot be reversed."

"Thor, your tone unnerves me," Sif said, looking up at him with a measured gaze. "Sága *has* done something that cannot be reversed. Asgardians lie dead in heaps. Those soldiers are more than just guards. They have names. Families. How can you call Sága righteous?"

Thor went to reply, but found that he didn't have an answer. At least not the one that Sif wanted to hear. She had refused to listen earlier when he'd cast blame toward Odin, and then himself, suggesting that there were plenty of Asgardians who suffered injustice who didn't carry out a killing spree. She was right, of course, but her reasoning did nothing to calm Thor's guilty heart.

"All good?" Tony Stark, who had been continuing his En-Trapp trials with Bruce Banner and Doctor Strange when Thor had arrived, called over to them from across the training room. He leaned on a cart of the En-Trapps, which silhouetted him with their colorful glow. Banner was tinkering with one of the devices next to him, but looked up at Thor, the worry blatant in his eyes. Thor could tell that his fellow Avengers knew that he was in the midst of a battle that could change the course of Asgard's future—and history—depending on which way it went. These were battles that the Avengers were used to fighting together, but with the Rainbow Bridge destroyed, Thor had no way to lead them into battle.

Yet.

"I hope so," Strange said. He turned to Thor and Sif, removing his glowing fingers from his temples. "I was able to use you two as a pair of homing beacons, reaching out to Asgard. The problem is that there is something within your realm working against me."

"Sága has the power to absorb a seemingly limitless amount of mystical energy," Sif offered. "It could be her standing in your way."

"It's true. Before destroying it, Sága sapped the entire Rainbow Bridge of its power, and raided my father's storage of magical items to grow even stronger," Thor said. "If she is aware of your presence, she could put up a fight that even the Sorcerer Supreme may not be able to withstand."

Strange raised both eyebrows.

"No offense," Thor added.

"Oh," Strange said, chuckling lightly. "No, no, none taken. I was trying to feel if that was the case, but—no, I don't feel any active resistance. It's as if Asgard itself is changing. It's made it very difficult to catch. Even when I'm there, I *can* start rebuilding the Rainbow Bridge, but that will take some time. If I'm going to get you there urgently, it'll take cruder magic."

Thor cracked his fingers. "I will take the crudest you have to offer."

Thor watched as Tony Stark strode over to them, shaking his head. "You know, in any other circumstance, I might have to call attention to what you just said, but you're having a rough day, so I'm going to let it slide." Tony looked toward the sky and let out a long whistle. "F.R.I.D.A.Y.! Time to suit up."

"Where are you going?" Thor asked, confused as Tony's latest Iron Man model zipped into the room in a smooth arc, gleaming with repulsor power.

"With you two," Tony replied. "To Asgard."

"This is not your battle, Iron Man," Sif cautioned. "Thor and I may well walk to our deaths. You would be wise to remain on Earth and prepare your Avengers if Asgard truly does fall."

Thor stepped forward, taking Tony's shoulder in his grasp as the Iron Man suit landed next to them. "Listen, my Brother. We have fought together countless times. I consider you as mighty a warrior as any of the greatest soldiers who fight for Asgard. But Sif speaks true, friend."

"Here's the thing," Tony said. He stepped toward the suit, which opened up for him, and casually stuck out his arms. With every motion, the suit followed, snapping into place around his body. "Sága can drain magic, right? There's no one *less* magical than me. I have the mystical energy of a glazed donut—and not the ones from that St. Mark's Place, those are obviously bewitched. I can bring firepower that she won't be able to co-opt. Plus, take a look at Stephen."

Thor watched as Doctor Strange paced the floor, murmuring to himself. Glowing, circular sigils flew around his hands, and the God of Thunder was unsure if this was Strange attempting various spells, or just the way that a sorcerer of his level kept his hands busy while thinking.

"He's going to crack it any second now," Tony said as the suit closed around him, only leaving his face mask up. "You and Sif just got your butts handed to you on a silver platter by this lunatic, and what, you're going to go back there again and somehow beat her this time? We do this Avengers style, man. You, me, Sif."

Sif walked up to them and stood by Thor's side. "You have convinced me, Iron Man," she said. "I fear that Thor will not be able to destroy Sága when the time comes, but I see no other recourse."

"Sif!" Thor said, but found no anger when she looked at him.

"I understand," Sif said. "My heart breaks for her. For *us*. But the woman back in Asgard is not our friend. She's been turned into something else."

"She's no demon," Thor said. "In my memories, when she returned from Niffleheim, I thought her possessed, but I was wrong."

"She received her ability to absorb mystical power from somewhere or someone," Sif said, "but even if the source isn't demonic, she has been driven mad by thousands of years of confinement to her tomb. Our friend is dead, Thor. There is nothing left within her but rage, and it will burn Asgard to its core if we allow it to go unchecked."

"Of course she has been driven mad," Thor said. "But if we give up on her once again, just as we did before—"

A sound like a roaring wave cut Thor off and, for a horrible moment, the God of Thunder flashed back to when he and Sif were overcome by the explosion of Bifrost energy. He lifted his hammer instinctually to defend himself, but saw then that the sound had come from Doctor Strange, who looked as if he were on fire. Flames of all colors of the rainbow licked around him, building into an aura.

"ASGARD!" Strange yelled in a bellow that shook the ground below them, sounding as if one hundred different voices were speaking at once. Thor watched in wonder as a glowing, gigantic, rainbow replica of Doctor Strange's face burst out of the flames and settled in the air, floating above them. The gigantic, flaming face opened its mouth and, to Thor's amazement, he saw that the mouth was a swirling portal of energy.

Doctor Strange stood behind the face, standing still, his eyes closed.

"Stephen!" Thor called. "What shall we do?"

"The Rainbow Bridge will be rebuilt in time," Strange spoke, both his own mouth and that of the gigantic, flaming head moving. "Sága wasn't able to drain all of it. I've latched onto the power of what remains, but it will take me weeks to reconstruct it. In the meantime, I can get you to Asgard, but I caution you, while I will aim you toward the remaining Bifrost energy as best I can manage, it will not be precise. I am well aware of the dangers of Asgard, and I must warn you that I cannot promise you won't appear in the middle of an active volcano."

Thor looked at Sif and Iron Man, both of whom seemed unfazed.

"At the moment, there are far more troubling things in the realm of Asgard than volcanoes, my friend," Thor said. "We will do it. I cannot thank you enough for your help, Stephen. If this is the last time we share words, know that I am in awe of your power and of you as a man. It has been a pleasure to be an Avenger alongside of you."

"Fight, Thor," Strange said. "Don't make me build us a bridge to your death."

Bruce Banner walked up to Thor, a look in his eyes that Thor recognized from all of the times they'd charged into battle together: fierce, unwavering loyalty. "I'm coming, too," Banner said.

"No, friend. You cannot," Thor replied. He pointed to Strange, whose body shuddered as another wave of flaming energy coursed through his body. "I do not know the extent of Sága's power. If she is able to somehow find Stephen's magic rebuilding the bridge in Asgard, she might be able to drain him as well—then we would all be doomed. If you see anything go wrong, I need you here to stop it."

Banner went to protest but paused, breathing in. Thor could see that Banner, brilliant as he was, knew that the Asgardian was right.

"Maybe you could use one of the En-Trapps," Tony said. "Throw one at Strange, lock him away for a bit so Sága can't get to him."

"These are now functional?" Thor asked, smiling as he gestured with his hammer toward the cart of lightly luminescent devices. He couldn't believe that he'd been testing them just days before.

"Mostly," Tony said. "They can contain a great deal of Strange's magic, but—you know what, we're delaying here."

"I fear that this is good-bye, Banner," Thor said. He

embraced his friend and then, avoiding Banner's eyes, parted from his friend and looked at Sif, who stood facing the glowing projection of Doctor Strange's face. As Thor and Iron Man lined up next to her, the mystical visage widened its mouth.

"Not a way I thought I'd be spending my day, doing a cannonball into Strange's mouth," Iron Man said.

Thor looked to Sif. "Are you ready?"

Sif nodded. "Are *you*, Thor?"

He closed his eyes, and when he did so, he saw the reflection of himself, Sif, and Sága in the pond near his quarters. They had been so young. It felt like another life.

"I am," Thor said, and stepped forward.

With Iron Man on his left and Sif on his right, Thor broke into a run, charging toward Doctor Strange's mystical projection. He felt hot energy wash over him as he dove in, instantly swept up in the spiraling power of the portal. Thor closed his eyes, knowing that when he opened them, he might be greeted by devastation.

CHAPTER THIRTEEN

REFLECTION

Sága looked down at Loki's still form, laid out on the ground, doll-like. A jagged chunk of the Obsidian Tablet was mystically bonded to his chest, glowing with his name. Feeling a swell of an emotion that she couldn't pinpoint as anything other than a deep, directionless loss, Sága knelt before Loki and traced her fingers along his cheekbone.

"Good-bye," she said softly, closing her eyes. As much as she hated him most of all for his betrayal, she couldn't imagine an Asgard without him. Soon, though, she wouldn't have to. When her crusade was done, and the rest of the surviving Asgardians lay on the stone floor with chunks of the Obsidian Tablet on their chests, forgotten to history as she had been, she would return to the place that started it all. The place where Odin bewitched her to live single days as years. The place where she'd encountered Laufey, the king of the Frost Giants and the true father of Loki, who had given her a means by which to carry out her revenge on Odin all those years ago—her power source.

She would return to Niffleheim and she would pay the price that Laufey promised her she'd have to pay if she ever used her newfound power. With every particle of mystical energy that she absorbed, she would lose a scrap of her immortal life. She felt the core, the glowing ember that she had swallowed at Laufey's behest all of those years ago, burning her from the inside out. It wouldn't be long now.

She wondered if Laufey still lurked in the depths of Hel, and if he'd be happy to know what she'd done. Though she knew that the wicked Frost Giant had only used her as a weapon in his lifelong grudge against Odin, Sága couldn't help but feel grateful to Loki's birth father. He'd found her beaten nearly to death after a Wyvern attack. Sága had crawled to the entrance to Hel, hoping she'd be let in. At least, then, she'd truly be dead. Instead of being greeted by Hela, it was Laufey who crept toward her from the shadows with that mystical well of power in the form of a blazing ember.

He listened to her plight and to her stories of Loki. He told her his own, of when the young Trickster was just an infant. He told her all about Odin, confirming all of her most hateful thoughts of the king who had condemned her to suffer in this wicked realm.

"Take this. I would do it myself, but the dead cannot withstand its power. It comes from the center of Hel's most blazing pit," Laufey said, pressing the scalding stone onto her tongue, "and you can be the Siphon. Use the power of Asgard against the realm itself, and then, when the time comes, then you will find peace. Do you want this?"

Sága swallowed, and Laufey grinned.

That was the only part of her story that her one-time friends would never know. As she knelt over Loki, stroking his cheek, she wondered how he'd react if she told him. At this point, he would probably try to save her from the certain death promised by the stone boring through her very soul, but she couldn't take it. Anything that Loki said to her was a lie. She knew now that he'd never loved her. He'd never loved anyone but himself.

A thunderous roar burst through the cavern, and, Sága momentarily feared the power center within was about to consume her. Yet, the sound didn't come from within her. It came from above.

A swirling, raging portal opened in the sky above, splintering the winding path that led back up to the mountain with its mystical aftershock. Sága squinted up at the rift and, to her shock, saw three figures leap out, speeding toward her.

"There goes the element of surprise," one of them said in a robotic tone.

"We must have been drawn to *her* Bifrost energy!" a familiar voice said—*Sif*. Somehow, Sif.

"It doesn't matter!" Thor's voice sounded. "ATTACK!"

"Impossible," Sága murmured. How could they have survived her onslaught at the Rainbow Bridge? She had hit them with almost all of Asgard's mystical power, all at once, and here they were hours later, charging into battle?

One of the figures, who was covered head to toe in gleaming scarlet and golden armor, rocketed toward her, glowing with some kind of mystical energy from within. The armored figure barreled into Sága with a power that startled her. Sága pushed her attacker away from her, but was instantly hit with a blast of lighting that made her muscles tighten and her bones shake within her body.

"Thor!" she spat, looking to the side as, indeed, the God of Thunder landed, with Sif by his side. They were burned, but not nearly as badly as they should've been. Indeed, Sága thought they had been reduced to ash.

"It seems the element of surprise might not be *entirely* gone," Thor said, swinging his hammer as he sped toward his former friend.

Sága whipped her head around to see the armored assailant walking toward her from the side, gauntlets glowing with blinding white energy. The energy shot toward her in a ray, which she rolled to avoid. Sága felt that the mystical energy she'd built was already being consumed by her power source within, which made her blood burn—a reminder that she had little time left. If she let this new attacker and her two old friends have the chance now, they just might be able to defeat her.

Sága bolted toward the armored foe who floated above her, dodging blasts of energy as she did so, as well as another charge of lightning as Thor and Sif ran toward her on the ground. Sága flung herself through the air and reached for the armored man, who saw what she was doing and turned to zip away.

"You're fast," a smooth voice came out from within. "I'm much faster—"

"No." Sága spun in midair and caught his metallic leg and, gritting her teeth, tapped into the very core of her stolen energy. Her insides ached as the power blasted out around her and into the armor, which burst off of her attacker in pieces like shattered glass. "You are *not.*"

"IRON MAN!" Thor called from below.

"A *man?*" Sága said with a laugh as a human, startled and afraid, fell down along with the scraps of his armor. He hit the ground with a satisfying breaking sound, and Sága landed powerfully next to him. "A human, Thor? This is what you bring to face me?"

"Tony!" Thor cried out, barreling toward Sága. He said the name as if the man were a friend.

Sága looked down at the unarmored human, increasingly amazed that he had been able to do what he did. Though it had, of course, come apart after her surge of power . . . perhaps there was, after all, something to that suit he wore.

Sága held her hands up and, calling on her last remaining

storage of energy, made the shards of armor float all around her. She willed it to snap to her arms, stretching and bending to her will as it began to rebuild into a complete suit of armor.

Thor and Sif skidded to a stop in front of her, as the suit began to, once again, glow with that blinding white energy. Sága, now wearing Iron Man's armor, let out a metallic laugh as she worked her magic through the system, using the ethereal power of the Bifrost to obliterate the strange programming that this Iron Man used to pilot his suit. Strange lines of light crossed her vision and, frustrated, she ripped off the helmet, throwing it to the ground.

Even if her own stolen power was depleted, she now had all she needed to finish Thor and Sif and complete her crusade. Soon, she knew that the sweet peace of death would come for her . . . but first, she had more damage to do.

Thor stared in horror at Sága, who flexed her fingers within Iron Man's suit. He couldn't tell if Tony was breathing from this distance, and that wasn't the only thing that made his chest swell with panic. All around the stony chamber were his people, the Warriors Three and his mother, hanging from the cavern wall by their hands and feet. He prayed they were unconscious.

When he, Sif, and Iron Man had burst from the portal,

he'd glimpsed Sága leaning over Loki's form, with Odin nearby as well, laid out on the ground. Thor didn't know if Sága had brought them here, to her longtime tomb, to kill them for the poetry of it or if she had a larger plan, but he knew now that Sif was right.

This was never going to be anything but a fight.

"Sága!" Thor bellowed, holding his hammer out to her. "Back away from him!"

She lifted her foot above Tony, positioning her boot above his neck. "Do you love this man, Thor? Do you care for him as you once cared for me? Let me show this little man exactly what happens to those who place their trust in *you*."

"I am SORRY!" Thor screamed.

Sága paused, her foot still positioned over Tony's neck. Thor's breath was ragged in his chest, as he knew he wouldn't be able to get Sága in time to get her away from his fallen friend. If she decided to do it, she could crush his throat in an instant.

"It is my fault," Thor said. He felt Sif's eyes on him, but prayed that she wouldn't act. He attempted to meet her gaze, to give her a *trust me* glance, but her eyes were locked on Sága and Tony.

"It's a little late for regrets," Sága snapped back. "Look at me now, Thor. The rivers of Asgard run red. You think me worse than anyone you've faced in battle. I can see it in your eyes."

"I don't," Thor said. "I know what happened to you now, and I swear to you, I will make it up to you. You can take your rightful place in Asgard and—"

"THERE IS NO ASGARD!" Sága snapped, and Thor gasped as she lowered her foot. Instead, though, she rested it on Tony's chest, pinning his unconscious form to the ground. "Look around you, old *friend*. Look and see what I've done!"

Thor's father and brother lay on the ground, their names glowing on the shattered slabs of stone. He thought about the shards of obsidian that covered this place when he and Odin first discovered Loki in Sága's vacant sarcophagus. There had been no name glowing on the stones in that moment.

Thor knew what to do.

Sága's eyes widened as Thor smiled. She glanced from Thor, to Odin and Loki, and let out a furious breath. She bounded toward Thor, seething. Thor knew that Sága was aware he'd figured it out, but she wouldn't get to him in time.

"LOKI!" Thor bellowed. "ODIN!"

"NO!" Sága screamed.

No sooner had he said the words than the black stone tablets on their chests burst into pebbles, the sound echoing through the cavern like a gunshot. Sága, in a panic, turned back toward them—but not fast enough.

In a flash, Loki was on her. She reached back to strike him, but he brought his hands down quickly, stabbing a shard of the Obsidian Tablet into her neck. The moment that Sága hit the ground, with Loki on her, Thor burst into action.

He looked over his shoulder to Sif, who was already running along with him toward the battle.

"Get Tony to safety!" he called to her. Thor kicked off the ground and took flight.

Thor rocketed toward Sága, who wrestled with Loki on the ground. As Thor lifted the hammer, Sága shot out a repulsor beam from Iron Man's suit, sending Loki flying across the cavern. Thor brought Mjolnir down on Sága's chest, attempting to crack the chest-piece repulsor, which was the source of the armor's power. She had clearly hijacked it with her siphoned magical powers, so Thor was certain that she'd be able to use the suit to some extent even if he hacked away at its energy source, but he again struck the repulsor with a mighty blow.

Sága tucked in her feet and shot them into Thor's chest, letting off a blast of energy from the suit. She skidded back into the wall and, as Thor flipped around in midair and flew back toward her, she grabbed the shard of the Obsidian Tablet deep in her neck and pulled it out. Blood flowed into the suit.

Thor landed in front of her, swinging the hammer, prepared to attack again. But now, Sága stood still, looking at

Thor with pure hatred. Thor glanced over his shoulder and saw Sif standing in front of Tony, who was now conscious and seemed to be trying to rejoin the fight, leaning over Sif's shoulder and cursing. Thor couldn't help but smile in spite of the situation.

"You remembered them," Sága spat, her face twisted into a sour expression. "I lay Forgotten for millennia, and you remembered Odin and Loki's names as if the Obsidian Tablet had never touched them. I truly meant so, so little to you all."

"I don't know what to tell you, Sága," Thor said. "I remember now. Perhaps the spell only affects those in Asgard at the time of its casting. Maybe it only works once. We may never know."

He looked skyward, and saw Frigga beginning to wake, still pinned to the cave's wall. The Warriors Three remained limp.

"You wanted to sentence *all* of Asgard to the fate you suffered?" Thor asked. "To be Forgotten to time?"

Sága stared at Thor, and nodded slowly. "That's it. You weren't in Asgard when I carved their names upon the stone. Of *course*."

Thor spun his hammer, feeling it build up energy. It felt ready to rip his hand off from the power it was gathering, but Thor knew that he might just have this one shot. As long as he could keep Sága talking and his own power building, he might have a shot at taking out that chest piece.

"It's cruel, what he did to you," Thor said. "Odin used you in an attempt to set Loki straight, and that was wicked. As wicked as any of the deeds you committed today, Sága, and perhaps more. He let you suffer in Niffleheim and, when you came back for vengeance, with these new powers of yours, he entombed you here and willed you out of existence. I cannot fault you for wishing to erase my father. Were I in your position, Sága, I might do the same. But Loki? What has Loki done to you?"

Sága tilted her head back as Thor continued to whirl his hammer.

"You loved him," Thor continued. "And he loved you, poor as he was at showing it. I can tell you of my memories that have been restored, friend. Loki wished to save you from Odin after your first attack. To stop him. It was *I* that failed you, Sága."

"Is he one of your friends, too?" Sága asked, still looking up.

"Loki?" Thor asked. "He and I are . . . estranged, but—"

"No," Sága said, looking at Thor with a serene smile, overcome with a sudden peace. "I mean the glowing man floating above the remains of the Rainbow Bridge."

Thor's eyes widened and, in a flash of blazing repulsor light, Sága rocketed upward, shooting out of the cavern. Thor released the hammer, which arched after her, but Sága was too fast, too powerful. Mjolnir burst through the stone path, sending jagged boulders raining down, but missed Sága entirely, as she wove up toward the distant exit.

"She feels Doctor Strange's presence," Thor said. "It's what I feared. She's going to try to absorb his power. And if she does—"

"No need to say it." Loki strode over to Thor, his eyes set in a determined glare. "She'll be unstoppable. We have to go, now."

Thor snatched Mjolnir out of the air, and instantly began to spin it again as Loki stood before him. Sif and Tony Stark watched from across the cavern, as Odin also rose to his feet with a pained groan.

"We?" Thor asked. "Loki, if you attempt to stop me, I'll have to—"

"I know we can't save her, Thor," Loki said, his eyes shining. Blood and sweat caked on his face, running in beads down his cheeks. "You can't do it alone. She doesn't care about you anymore—she has nothing but hatred for you and Odin at this point. It's me that she loves as much as she hates."

"As ever, you ride the line, Loki," Odin said. He nodded to Thor, whose muscles tensed as his father stared at him. "Stop her, my Sons."

Thor glared at Odin without saying a word. He was tempted to turn Mjolnir toward him, and show him just how much he cared for the king's fatherly advice at the moment.

"Go now, Thor," Sif said. "I will release the Warriors Three and we will make our way there."

"I will call for my craft, so that we may journey with haste," Odin said.

"And, uh, I'll be here wishing that I never came here at all," Tony said. "Sorry about that."

"No," Thor said. "You might have saved us all, Tony."

"How?" Tony asked.

"If Sága had all the power she needed to defeat us, she would not have wanted the suit," Thor said. "She would not be headed toward Doctor Strange right now. She's near depletion and we know that now. This is a battle that we can win."

Thor looked to Loki, holding his brother's gaze. Loki's sweaty black hair moved in the wind created by Thor's rotating hammer. In all of the many years that Thor had known and loved and hated and feared his brother, he had never seen Loki so broken.

He held out his hand for Loki to take.

"Together," Thor said.

Loki hesitated for a moment and then, nodding, took Thor's hand in his own. Thor pointed the hammer upward and the two brothers burst out of the mountain with a brilliant flash of lighting.

CHAPTER FOURTEEN

TOGETHER

As Thor and Loki blazed through the air, together, directed by the power of Mjolnir, they shot toward the ruins of the Rainbow Bridge. In the distance, Thor saw that Sága had already landed in front of Heimdall's Observatory, where the gigantic mystical projection of Doctor Strange's face floated. Rainbow energy had been flowing out from the projection's eyes, slowly rebuilding the fractured bridge, which ended in a splintered plateau of empty, powerless crystal mere yards after the observatory.

However, Sága now stood in the bath of rainbow energy that the projection of Stephen Strange's eyes released, her hands reaching toward him. Strange's face contorted, trying to free itself from Sága's siphoning power, but she was already too strong. She glowed brilliantly, her entire body beginning to give off a blinding luminescence.

"It's too late," Loki hissed as they got closer. "She's got him!"

"Indeed," Thor said. "But, she doesn't see *us*. If I let you go, will you land safely?"

"Ah, there's that brotherly concern," Loki snapped. "Of course I will."

"Meet me up there," Thor said.

"It'll be an *interesting* death, at least," Loki said, and jumped away from Thor, descending through the sky. He whipped his cape around and, in a swirl of green, disappeared.

Thor continued his descent toward Sága and reached back his hammer, closing his eyes. He silently called on all of the powers of Asgard, willing the skies above to lend him their power like never before. Clouds gathered in the sky, blotting out all light around them except for the glow that came from Sága and Doctor Strange below. As Thor got closer and closer, he held his hammer high and thunder boomed, shaking what felt to be the entire realm.

The sky surged with lighting that burst from the clouds, veining down toward Thor's hammer. As bolt after bolt hit the hammer, Mjolnir glowed so blindingly bright that it made even Thor's eyes water.

As Thor rocketed down, Sága looked up, her pale face bathed in the light of the enormous, spiraling lighting blast that shot from Thor's hammer.

The surging bolt hit Sága directly in the middle of the repulsor on her chest, which shattered, sending a secondary surge of power through the suit. For a moment, the entire suit charged up with incredible, white hot power, and a knot of panic formed in Thor's chest as he landed on the observatory.

She shot her gauntlets forward, and sent a horrific mixture of lightning and repulsor power back toward Thor, who met it with another powerful blast from Mjolnir. The two blazing attacks met in midair, forming a stalemate.

"IT'S OVER, THOR!" Sága shouted. "TIME TO—"

A flash of green appeared between Sága and Thor, in the center of their attacks. Thor watched as Sága's eyes widened and, as horror dawned over her face, he knew what had happened.

Both Sága and Thor ended their blasts at once, as a charred Loki teetered on the observatory between them.

Doctor Strange's face, still convulsing from Sága's attack floated above them, their only source of light as they watched Loki crumple below them.

Thor, his heart hammering in his chest, hung back as Sága let out a pained cry and threw herself to the ground, skidding over to Loki. Smoke rose from his body, which looked burned and tattered beyond repair. It was unbelievable, with his charred flesh and visible bone, that he could even reach up to take Sága's hand as she held him.

"Why would you do that!?" she snapped, shaking him. "I never meant for you to die! Why in the name of Asgard would you do that?"

"*You'd rather me be Forgotten?*" Loki croaked. "*Is that not worse?*"

Thor watched trembling, as Sága leaned in to Loki, letting out a howl of rage and sorrow.

"I-I don't know!" Sága screamed. "I could have never—wouldn't have—Loki, you wretched, selfish, craven fool. After all of this, after everything that you did to me, you force me to watch as you die by my hand?" She held his charred form to her armored body, tears spilling down her face. "How could you do this?"

Thor pointed his hammer behind Sága, letting out a powerful blast of lightning. Loki, not a single burn mark on his skin, appeared behind Sága with a sword, which caught the power of Thor's lightning on the blade.

"I never meant to, love," Loki said, and stabbed the blade, coursing with the power of Thor's lightning, through Sága's back. As the sword burst out through her chest, Iron Man's armor fell off of her in pieces.

Thor, his throat tight, watched with great sadness as Sága, confused, looked from the real Loki behind her, to the burned, skeletal duplicate in front of her that fell to ash. She let out a weak croak in response, as Loki stood over her. He grabbed the hilt of the sword, pushing it farther in.

"You're right. I *have* spent an inordinate amount of time honing my trickery," he said. "I probably would've been able to find you if I knew to look. But I didn't know. I forgot, you see. Your crusade is over, Sága."

Thor looked at them, and, for a moment, imagined them younger, sitting on the bridge that had once stood here, holding hands and sharing secrets. He wished he would have known the horror that one of those very secrets would bring to all of their lives.

But that wasn't the way this story was going to go. They all played their part in the way things had turned out and, as he stared at Sága, bleeding sparkling, mystically enhanced blood on the end of Loki's sword, he realized that there was nothing left to say. No promises to make to Sága about redemption, no apologies that would make it all better. All he could say was the truth, which he would now have to hold for the rest of his life.

"I love you, Sága," Thor said, lifting his hammer above her.

She looked up at him, her wild eyes narrowing into slits. Through the obvious pain, she choked out a response.

"No," she rasped. "You *don't*."

In a great, final burst of energy, Sága leapt into the sky in a great arc, still impaled by the sword. She held out her arms in a great dive, reaching for Doctor Strange's projection. Thor and Loki watched in amazement and horror as she disappeared into the projection's swirling portal mouth.

"Oh no," Thor whispered.

The projection contorted, flashing brightly white, and Thor knew that the power was about to be cut off. He grabbed Loki by the shoulder and ran forward with his brother in tow.

Loki pointed behind them. "They're coming."

In the distance, Thor saw Odin's crafts headed their way. That meant that the Warriors Three had been risen, and reinforcements were coming.

"We have no time," Thor said and, hoping he wouldn't regret it, pulled Loki close to him and threw himself back through the portal of Doctor Strange's projection.

Sága landed in front of a man whose face matched the glowing visage that had appeared before Heimdall's Observatory. He stood in a velvety blue garment and a flowing cape, looking at her through glaring eyes. Shifting his hands forward, his hands formed glowing sigils that blazed with mystical symbols that she didn't recognize.

"Sága," the man said, staring down at her.

"Giant, glowing face," she said, reaching backward. Her hands found the hilt of the sword.

The man walked slowly around her, prepared to attack at any moment. Sága wondered how powerful he was. In any case, she knew she'd find out when she sapped him of his energy. If that wasn't enough to return to Asgard and, once and for all, complete her retribution, she didn't know what was. With images of Loki's body falling to ashes before her, she found that her anger, along with her physical pain, had expanded.

"In the past," she said, pulling the sword out of her back, "I would tell you that I have no quarrel with you, sorcerer. But you know Thor. You helped him and his wicked brother Loki *trick* me."

"I did not know their plan," the man said. "But you're right—I fight for Thor on this day. This isn't a fight you want, Sága."

"It's not a fight I want. It's that beautiful glow within you. Let's see how much power you have to offer," Sága said, lifting the bloody sword high and charging toward the sorcerer.

He blasted her with the circle of magic, which expanded around her like a hoop and looped her in. It squeezed shut around her, a physical force, and spun her around the room like a child's toy. But now that she'd stolen some of the Bifrost energy that the sorcerer had re-created, she had enough power to burst out again.

Just in time to come to a stop in front of a giant, green, hulking monster.

Thor and Loki emerged from the portal, landing together in Stark Tower's training room just in time to see the Hulk lift Sága by the foot, swinging her around like a rag doll. He slammed her into the cushioned wall over and over as Doctor Strange, floating into the air on a disc of violet magical energy, approached, holding his hands up high. Hulk had his own plans for Sága, though. He continued to bash her into the wall, bouncing her over and over again.

"I hate when he does that," Loki said.

Thor led the charge toward Sága, noticing that the bloody sword was discarded off to the side.

"Now!" Thor said, leaping into the air as Hulk let Sága fly across the room.

"Careful, fool!" Loki said. "She can heal! If she's absorbed more power, she may be at her peak again."

Thor met Sága in midair and slammed his hammer down on her, letting loose a brilliant blast of lightning. Sága caught it in her bare hands, blood still flowing from her chest, and laughed as Thor pushed toward her.

"I thought you'd want to die on Asgard!" Sága roared.

"I attempted to give you the same courtesy," Thor replied, sending more power toward her. Doctor Strange and the Hulk barreled toward Sága, ready to unleash their own forces.

"NO!" Sága bellowed, her entire body glowing with blinding Bifrost energy. "THIS IS BETWEEN ME AND ODIN'S SONS!"

She screamed and unleashed a tremendous, overwhelming wave of energy. Thor, for a nightmarish moment, thought that she'd sent him through another Bifrost explosion, but this was nothing like that. Hot power burst up under him, ripping up the flooring that Tony Stark told them was unbreakable. Hulk, Doctor Strange, Loki, and Thor himself were caught in the wave of pure, unfiltered power that Sága released toward them.

The cart of En-Trapps whipped across the room and smacked into Loki, sending the devices scattering across the ruins of the floor as they fell.

Thor hit the ground hard, and Loki went tumbling. The En-Trapps rolled across the floor like marbles.

Sága stalked toward Loki.

Thor reached out and grabbed an En-Trapp. It glowed a bright emerald green. *Appropriate.*

Sága lifted Loki by the neck. The Hulk stirred off to the side, and Doctor Strange screamed in pain under the green beast's weight.

"It makes a kind of poetic sense," Sága said, squeezing her fingers into Loki's throat. He let out a pained choke, but she didn't cease. "We will both die today, Loki. Something tells me I'll see *you* in the place that waits beyond."

Thor stood, the En-Trapp in his hands, facing Sága with glistening eyes. He stared at her until she turned to look at him with a scowl.

"*What?*" she snapped. "You're next, Thor. Let us have this moment."

"Sága . . ."

"LET US HAVE THIS MOMENT!" Sága screamed.

"Look around you. Look at what I've already done. What other way do you see this going, Thor? Give your brother the one thing you never offered when you were boys, and certainly not since. Give him *peace*."

Thor reeled back his hand.

"I really do love you, Sága," he said, and flung the En-Trapp at her. It blossomed as it shot toward her, its metallic flaps sparkling with green energy like some kind of dazzling, otherworldly flower. With incredible speed, certainly improved from the last test run that Thor had tried with it, the En-Trapp snapped into place around Sága, who began to glow with rainbow power.

"What is—" Sága's voice was muffled as the device fitted itself around her face, expanding.

Loki fell at her feet as she stumbled backward.

As Sága began to glow like a being made from pure energy, the En-Trapp compressed, pushing in on her. Thor winced as the device crunched its parts together, condensing the energy that Sága had become. It contorted and reshaped itself, struggling to contain her until, as a final, anguished cry came from within, the En-Trapp snapped to its normal size and snap.

The spherical device hit the ground and twitched, flashing emerald, and then fell still, and didn't glow at all.

Thor stood, silently mourning, as Loki peered down at the En-Trapp as, behind him, the Hulk shifted back to Banner, who helped the injured Doctor Strange to his feet.

Blood flowing down his neck, Loki looked up at Thor. "Is she dead?"

"She lives," Thor shook his head. "The device is meant to condense energy. If we were to open it, she would reform as we left her. I believe she is in stasis."

"She's in pain," Loki said, looking down in horror at the En-Trapp. "H-How can we keep her in there?"

Thor stared at his brother, wishing he had consoling words to share. He thought back to that once lost memory in Odin's corridor, when Loki called Thor to action, pleading with him to help stop Odin from killing Sága. Thor had given Loki no comfort then, and though he didn't have an answer now, he thought long and hard about his response and, looking into his brother's gaze, Thor sighed.

"Would you rather her die, Loki?" Thor asked.

"No."

"Then, together, we will figure out what to do with her, in time," Thor said. "For now, Brother, I don't believe she is hurting anymore."

"This makes us no better than Odin," Loki said.

"It is on us, then, to reject his path," Thor said. "Sága will never be forgotten again, nor will she remain in her prison indefinitely. We will find another way."

"And if there isn't one?"

Thor looked at his brother, who stared back at him

fiercely. Loki's chin trembled as he gritted his teeth.

"There has to be," Thor said softly.

Thor and Loki stood above the En-Trapp, looking down at the device that, somehow, contained someone they once considered a friend. Thor hoped that the words he spoke to Loki were true—because then, at least *one* of them was no longer in pain.

EPILOGUE

ATONEMENT

The next day, back in the eternal realm of Asgard, Thor sat on the observatory with Heimdall behind him. The two watched as the projection of Doctor Strange's face slowly but surely re-created the Rainbow Bridge. Piece by small piece, the Bifrost stretched out before them, the colorful energy beginning to stir within.

"Your friend is a force of life unlike any other human I've met," Heimdall marked.

"Doctor Strange is impressive indeed," Thor said. "However, have you seen Tony Stark eat? He hasn't left the dining hall since Loki and I returned. I told him that I can take him back to Midgard whenever he's ready, but it appears that his stomach has a capacity unknown to Asgardians."

Heimdall smiled, but it did not reach his starry eyes. He stared out at the jagged Bifrost and sighed deeply.

"I did not call you here, Thor, to talk about your Midgardian friends," Heimdall said, "but to make good on a promise."

"Aye?"

"You asked me some time ago to alert you if I spied Loki," Heimdall said. "Indeed, I have."

"He disappeared the moment I returned with Sága, but that is to be expected," Thor said. "I will let Loki live in peace for now. I doubt, after what happened with Sága, he's altogether interested in mischief."

"I thought you might think so," Heimdall said, stepping back into the darkness of the observatory. "Maybe you'd rather ask him yourself."

Thor narrowed his eyes and peered into the shadows into which Heimdall had disappeared. Squinting, he looked for Loki, but saw no one. "Heimdall? Do you speak nonsense? Where is—"

"Never see what's right in front of your nose, do you?"

Loki appeared next to Thor, his legs hanging over the edge of the Bifrost. He stared ahead as Thor's eyes rested upon him.

Something about Loki looked different.

"Brother," Thor said, careful to keep his tone measured. Circumstances had brought them closer together and pushed them further apart in the past, but if there was one thing that Thor could be certain of with Loki, it was that there was *nothing* he could be certain of. For all he knew, when night came and went, Loki could've sparked up the belief that this was all Thor's fault. Thor wasn't entirely sure that he'd disagree, either.

"Thor," Loki said, still looking away.

Thor forced a smile. "Look at us, Loki. This is silly. Come with me, back to the kingdom. Let us converse like brothers."

"What punishment does Odin face?" Loki asked.

Thor's smile faded. "It is complicated, Brother. You know that. Odin claims to be sorry for what he did, but he sits on the throne nonetheless. He and I have not spoken since my return. I have no words to spare."

"I have words," Loki said, his eyes flashing. "Oh, do I have words."

A heavy silence fell between them. Together, for a time, they watched the glistening shards of Bifrost grow, slowly, almost unnoticeably, repairing itself.

"You won't believe me," Loki said, "but on Midgard, when I clashed with the Hood and those other fools . . . my plan was not to team up against you."

Thor met Loki's eye, but didn't respond.

"You may think me a schemer above all, Thor. An opportunist. And perhaps you're right," he said. "But know this: above all, I am a watcher. I listen and I see. There is something happening on Midgard, and not just with the Hood and his little team. Great forces are gathering to bring down the Avengers—and you, Thor, are seen as the number one target."

"And you didn't wish to join these forces?" Thor asked.

"I don't wish to see you dead," Loki said. "Not anymore. If I did, you wouldn't be breathing. But . . ."

"Always. Always a but."

"I will tell you this, Thor, and do not ask for more information than I can give," Loki said. "The Hood is not who I was worried about. His cloak no longer answers to him . . . and word is spreading. There are forces that seek to control the demon that once inhabited that garment. Should it fall into the wrong hands—"

"And you suggest that *yours* are the right hands? You tell me that you mean to protect me from evil forces only to later suggest that your goal was to obtain the Hood's cloak," Thor said. "I cannot trust you, Brother."

"Then trust this," Loki said. "Keep your eyes open. Trouble is brewing. Trouble that neither you nor I can withstand."

Thor held his gaze.

"Or, maybe I wanted the cloak to myself," Loki said, grinning widely. "You just don't *know*, do you, Thor? How very sad for you."

After a moment of tense silence, for the first time in a long time, the two brothers laughed together.

"One more thing, Loki. If you didn't want to kill me, as you say, then why unleash Sága? I know that you said her name. You called her forth."

"I didn't know what was within the casket," Loki said. He smiled a little in spite of himself. "Just that Odin wanted nothing more than to hide the truth. If you don't believe me now, Thor, at least believe this: I once thought you and Odin to be the same. Immovable, prideful, arrogant, and cruel. I may not *like* you, Thor, but you are nothing like our father."

Thor opened his mouth to respond but, with a soft gust of wind, Loki was gone.

The rest of that night felt to Thor like a dream. He ate with Tony Stark, laughed with the Warriors Three, shared secret jokes with Sif, and held his mother close, happy beyond belief that she was now free of the burden of truth that Odin had laid upon her. He'd had no idea how much it wore on her. As they feasted, Asgardians all around stood up to share stories about their friends and family lost in Sága's crusade. Now, those soldiers had joined the legends of Asgard, never to be forgotten.

Thor lifted his goblet each time, echoing the call of those around him. "May Valhalla welcome them."

As the festivities wore on, and Tony bragged about what percentage of the En-Trapp was his idea—which, Thor knew but didn't say, Doctor Strange, who had added a powerful hex into Banner's coding, might contest—Thor looked up and noticed Odin, who had been silent all night, lean over to Frigga and whisper something in her ear. She nodded and stood, helping the injured king to his feet.

Thor watched as Frigga saw Odin to the door, and then parted from him. Odin disappeared into the hall.

Thor narrowed his eyes, standing.

"Hey, where are you going?" Tony asked, biting off a chunk from a big, meaty drumstick. "I was just getting to the part where you blasted all of Banner's En-Trapps to pieces."

Thor feigned a smile. "I'll be back, friends. Tell your tales, Stark—tall as they may be."

Thor walked away amidst Tony's protests and toward the door, where Frigga stood. She turned to meet Thor with a stern face.

"Leave him," Frigga said. "He mourns, too."

Thor embraced his mother. "I'm certain he does. But he and I must share words."

Frigga pursed her lips and then, after a second of thought, nodded. Thor touched her cheek and then turned down the dark hall. He walked into the throne room, expecting to see Odin seated upon the high chair, but found that it was empty.

Following a hunch, he continued through the room, and down the corridor toward Odin's personal treasure trove, which Sága had violated, and where the En-Trapp that contained her essence was now housed, guarded by the rebuilt Destroyer.

There Odin was, at the end of the hall, leaning against the corridor wall.

Thor, slowly and quietly, walked until he stood before Odin, whose gaze was cast downward.

"I imagine you loathe me," Odin said.

Ignoring the remark, Thor gestured to the vault. "Were you going here to take her away again? To make us all forget?"

Odin looked up at Thor, his single eye glassy. "Do you think I would?"

Thor let his silence provide the answer.

"No," the All-Father murmured. "No, that is not why I'm here. Do you remember what happened here, so many years ago, in this very hall?"

Thor nodded.

"I had a chance, then," Odin said. "Sága had been stopped and we knew of her incredible powers. But she was *done*, Thor. I knew that I could kill her, or let her live and risk the people of Asgard again. I knew, then, that I'd made a mistake in my initial punishment for her. It was harsh beyond measure, all because I was searching for outside blame for Loki's actions. I blamed you, and Loki himself, and Sága . . . all but myself."

"Then why would you go on to sentence her to the worst fate imaginable? You've killed for less than what she did."

"If I sentenced her to death, I knew for certain that we'd lose Loki," Odin said. "If I let her live, I feared she'd corrupt Loki. I knew of this way, this old way, a last resort that my father confided in me as a young boy. On his word, I built the cavern that housed the Obsidian Tablet, and I prayed that I would never use it. But I did."

Thor narrowed his eyes. "Do you regret it?"

"Yes," Odin said, closing his eye. He breathed out a shaky breath, his lower lip trembling. "And no."

Thor took a step toward Odin, feeling his fist tighten as if on its own accord. "*What?*"

"I did what I did for Loki," Odin said. "And—I won't lie—for myself. I wanted to purge Asgard of the memory of what she did. Of what I did. I didn't think I could continue as king with this on my shoulders, so I did it. I can't take it back, Thor, and it would be a lie to say that I should have known better. I did what I did . . . because I am who I am. I want to believe that, should the same happen now, I would act with the empathy that you deservedly expect from me." He looked up at Thor, a tear spilling from his eye, into his white beard. "But I don't know if I would, Son."

Thor unclenched his fist.

"What are we going to do about her now?" Thor asked.

"I leave that to you," Odin said. "If you wish for my guidance, Thor, it is yours. But I leave it to you."

Thor closed his eyes, and the feeling of hot, overwhelming hatred slowly dissipated. He didn't know when he'd be able to look upon his father with loving eyes again, but the man's confession had, at least, inspired Thor to offer his own.

"She wanted me to tell you," Thor said. "When Loki, as a boy, was planning to act out with his trick, Sága came to me, but urged me to tell you. I didn't. I wanted to settle it myself. I thought I was acting as a king would."

Thor walked away from Odin, but stopped when his father spoke again.

"It is hard, being king," Odin said. And then, after a short pause, he added, "But I imagine you will be a far better one than I."

Thor looked back over his shoulder at the old man who had given him life, power, and so much more. He prayed that one day he would be able to see past how much Odin had taken as well.

"I hope so, Father."

Thor left Odin in the hallway and walked out of the palace, toward the pond by his quarters. No sooner did he sit in front of the water than he heard a rustle in the distance.

Thor looked up and, in the darkness of the woods across the pond, saw a tall figure with long black hair staring at him. He stood up, took a step forward, and saw Loki standing in the distance, watching him. The water stretched between the two brothers, standing across from each other, not moving.

Thor opened his mouth to greet his brother, but realized there was no need. He softly inclined his head, and Loki did the same. Thor lowered himself back onto the grass and looked down at the pond, where he saw his brother's reflection disappear back into the darkness of the woods. Thor peered into the glassy surface of the water, where his reflection was now alone. He remembered the image of Sága's youthful face staring back at him. It hurt but, for a moment, Thor allowed himself to smile at the memory.

Even with what happened, even with the path of uncertainty ahead, it wasn't all bad. It wasn't nearly all bad.

ACKNOWLEDGMENTS

This was a difficult book to write. While building the story, there was a lot going on in my life, and I thought it was those big, shifting, defining moments I was going through that made this story hard to write. That was all part of it of course, but the truth is a little stranger: I cared deeply about this story.

Thor is my favorite super hero for reasons that I won't get into, mostly because I hope I've illustrated them in this novel. Loki is my favorite super villain as well. I'd written Thor before in my Iron Man and Avengers novels, but to live in his world and get in his head, I knew I wanted to build a story that lived up to the Thor epics that I loved. I wanted it to mean something to me.

I've been thinking a lot about how many varied lives we live. I am not who I was when I was ten, or sixteen, or twenty-four. My surroundings, the people I know and love, the things I hold dear—so much of it changes. Maybe it's because I've moved a lot, but I tend to think that's a universal thing. It's so easy to forget how strongly you've felt for someone, for time to stretch between you like an endless bridge. A bridge that you could cross at any time, but don't. *Marvel Thor: Crusade of the Forgotten* is about forgetting who you were and, as a result, forgetting who you are now. It's also about the painful, graceful, cathartic process of realizing that your father is both fallible and mortal . . . even if he is a god.

Beyond all of the serious stuff, I want to thank Joe Books and Marvel for letting me make Thor *funny*. I remember sitting on a panel with a team of writers, a few of them industry legends and more than two who had written Thor, discussing the way humor and super-hero comics coexist. I don't know how it came up, but I said that Thor was the funniest super hero . . . and the panel looked at me as if I was crazy! I believe that I justified it and swayed them (maybe) but that goes to show how wide Thor's appeal is. In various generations, in many different stories, Thor has been a golden god, unknowable to us; he has been the most human of us all; he has been a fish out of water, stumbling through Earth and laughing at his mishaps. From the stellar movies (along with Avengers, the best of the Marvel Studios franchises by my estimation) to J. Michael Straczynski's transformative run, to Kieron Gillen's formative *Journey into Mystery*, to Jason Aaron's current epic, to all of the classics by Walt Simonson and the many, many greats who have contributed to the legacy, Thor has made me laugh, he has inspired me, and he has brought me to tears. He has given me great stories, and I've tried my best to give him one in return.

Acknowledgments

Thanks to everyone at Joe Books, especially Deanna McFadden for her empathy for creators and passion for stories. Thanks to Steve Osgoode for letting me continue to tell stories that mean the world to me. Thanks to Emma Hambly and Rebecca Mills for guidance, and to everyone at Marvel for your work as well. Finally, a big thank you to my wife, Amy, for her endless love and support.

I write this from San Diego, as Amy sleeps. Tomorrow, we'll board a plane and leave this city behind and return home. I write this so that, when I pick up this book in the years to come, I will remember how it felt to be alive, right now. Because these are days that I'd hate to forget.

Pat Shand
October 2017

ABOUT THE AUTHOR

PAT SHAND writes comics (*Destiny NY, Vampire Emmy, Clonsters*), novels (Iron Man, Avengers, Guardians of the Galaxy), and more. He lives in New York with his wife, Amy, and their army of cats. Follow him @PatShand pretty much everywhere.